Downtown boy.
Author: Herrera, Juan Felipe.
Reading Level: 3.7
Point Value: 4
Accelerated Reader Quiz #102422

DOWNTOWN BOY

JUAN FELIPE HERRERA

SCHOLASTIC PRESS
NEW YORK

LIBRARY OF CONGRESS CATALOGING-IN-PUBLICATION DATA

Herrera, Juan Felipe.

Downtown boy / by Juan Felipe Herrera. — 1st ed.   p.   cm.

Summary: From June of 1958 to June of 1959, Juanito tries to stay out of mischief and
be good as he, his mother, and his father move around the state of California, never
quite feeling at home.

ISBN 0-439-64489-5 (hardcover : alk. paper)

1.   Mexican Americans—Juvenile fiction.   [1. Mexican Americans—Fiction.
2. California — History — 1950 — Fiction.]   I. Title.   PZ7.H432135Dow 2005
[Fic]—dc22   2005002877

10   9   8   7   6   5   4   3   2   1   05   06   07   08   09

Printed in the United States of America   37
First edition, November 2005

The text type was set in 11.5-pt Augereau
Book design by Richard Amari

For Margarita.

For my daughter, Almasol Herrera-Mansour, and her class at Culver City High School, for Ashley and Erin Robles, for Arissa Navarro, for my alma mater, San Diego High, Las Cuatro Milpas and all the children in Logan Heights, San Diego and Lake Geneva Middle School, Wisconsin, for all the students in the Mission District and Chinatown, San Francisco, my ESL pals in Fresno, Mendota, Fowler, Huron, and Riverside, California, El Paso, Texas, Mesa, Arizona, New York City, Iowa City, and Jackson Hole High School, Wyoming.

For Kendra Marcus, my agent extroardinaire.

For Liz Szabla and Jennifer Rees, my editors with diamond eyes.

For my children, Joshua, Joaquín, Roberto, Marlene.

For Don Luis Leal, pioneer.

For Gregory Nava and Barbara Marinez-Jitner.

In memory of my father, Felipe, and dear mother, Luchita, who blazed the first downtown street that led to this path.

For uncles Roberto and Fernando and aunts Albina, Aurelia, and Teresa, RIP.

For Maria #7, wherever you are.

Love me tender…
Elvis, 1956

Juanito was movin', always movin'
Down the bumpy road, over here, over there
In the winds, around the sharp corner
Like a kite flappin' everywhere
For a little while he lived in the south
Then north, boom-bam, or was it nowhere?

YOU'RE GONNA KNOCK OUT SWEET PEA PRICE!

June 1958

YOU'RE GONNA KNOCK OUT SWEET PEA PRICE!

"Tonight, Juanito,"
my cousin Chacho tells me,
"you're gonna knock out Sweet Pea Price
at the Mission District Branch Boys Club
on Alabama Street!
You're gonna love boxing!

"You're the new dog in town, Juanito!
The tallest, slickest, and most of all — my *primo,*
the toughest cat on Harrison Street!"

"I, I, uh, Chacho,
don't know about . . . box —"

"Come on, Juanito;
I'm counting on you.

"With these giant fluffy gloves Coach Egan
makes us wear, nothing will hurt anyway.
I'll tell him to start you slow, maybe
in the third set, when the guys
are tired as rag dolls. Boxing's cool!

It's like doing the cha-cha-cha
with my papa's fat flour tortillas
baked around your knuckles!

"Show me your knuckles! Yeah, well,
like that. Okeh? You're gonna flatten 'em.
I promise, *Primo*."

"Chacho," I say, "I, uh, don't think my mom
likes me doing stuff like that and . . .
Papi said, back in Ramona Mountain,
that I shouldn't fight and that —"

"*Primo,* listen.
You're in The City now!
Big San Francisco.
In the Mission District. Okeh?
Not sissy Ramona Mountain!

"The Mission is the baddest and most
meanest and coolest
part of town. Just fifteen
minutes south from downtown
on bus number fourteen and
another fifteen
from the Golden Gate. Got it?"

"The number what?"

"Forget it," Chacho says.
"You're the tallest. Okeh?
Get with it, *Primo!*
Get tough, *Primo!*

"Tonight, Juanito,
at the Mission District Branch
Boys Club on Alabama Street
you're gonna get your welcome party.

"You wanna be a chump
or a champ?"

"Hey *Primo,* hurry. It's almost
six thirty!"

I bump into the pool tables, shuffle
through the gym doors. "This place smells like potatoes,
vinegar, and socks, huh?" I whisper.

"Stop draggin' your feet!" Chacho says,
pulling me forward.

"My cousin Juanito can whip Sweet Pea
in one round!" Chacho barks at the guys.
They stop and float toward me
in their tattered T-shirts and thin blue shorts.
They move in and move out
as if trying to feel if I am made out of
red bones of fire or if I am a boy made
of see-through ice sticks.

"One?" I ask Chacho. "You said
one round? But I never, Papi said, that —"

"You're the biggest dude
at The Club. Number one!" Chacho shouts

as he wraps a towel around my shoulders
and pushes the guys to one side.
"Number two! When school starts in September,
at Bryant Elementary, everyone will know
who's the boss. Number three!
No one will touch you. Not even
Geronimo Cadena, the Charley Horse champ.
Hurry, Juanito; swear —

"you're as slow
as the scarecrow in *The Wizard of Oz!*
But you're gonna get tough tonight.
At seven sharp!"

JUST LIKE THAT

Chacho pulls me to the corner.
"See Sweet Pea there?
On the other side of the mat.
He's laughing. But that means he's scared.
Okeh?

"When Coach Egan steps to the mat,
that means you got about five minutes.

"Coach was a sergeant
in the army.

"Hey! What are you doing
playing with your shoelaces?
Listen to me, Juanito!

"When Coach Egan says, 'If you cry,
you're mine,' it means
it's better to die on the mat
with all your guts
hangin' from your skinny ribs
and your jawbone danglin'
from your neck like a pair of skates
than have to go

to the office upstairs and
deal with the Sarge.

"When Coach starts making
announcements, you'll have about
one minute.

"Then, Sweet Pea will stand up,
you'll stand up. You'll have these gloves on, *Primo.*
Then,
you start throwing!

"Every time Sweet Pea swings, just duck!
Swish-swoop! Jus' like that.
And sneak in a fast hook, boom!
Don't ever hold back, 'cause

"if there's one thing Sweet Pea is good for,
it's eating you up if you just stand there like a noodle.
Here comes Coach. Ready?
Boom! Jus' like that."

ALL YOU GOT

Teeny
Cousin Chacho counts down and bounces his shiny head
back and forth, grins, and punches out air from his nostrils
like he's a tiny bull; then he slicks back the Vaseline goop
on his hair that he poured on this morning after Aunt Albina
made us ham and cheese *tortas.* She made them in her deli
downstairs, on Harrison Street, for me and all my seven cousins,
leftovers from making lunch for the guys across 20th Street
who work at Bekins Storage and Regal Pale Brewery. Wish
I was like Chacho. He bugs me, but he knows a lot about
San Francisco; he calls it The City. Now he presses back the
gooey stuff on his head. *Heh-heh,* his head looks like a goose.

"Hey you, Cadena, listen up!
Or you gonna give Sarge five
push-ups on your knuckles?

"Got a few announcements, boys,
before we begin the new season.
Cadena, what did I say?
Give me ten, right now!

"You the new guy?"
Coach comes at me for a second while Cadena
grunts and laughs at the same time.

"Uh, yes sir, Coach,
uh, Sarge, uh, Mister Egan . . . uh . . ."

"Make up your mind, boy.
Are you Whinnytoe, Chacho's cousin?

"You from Argentina, right?
Sound like you're from, uh . . .
Cuba? What country did you say you from?"

"Uh, here . . . uh . . . a little town, Fowler,
by Sanger, Fresno . . . uh . . . California."

"Never mind.
Rule number one —
I don't want any trouble.
You understand. And I don't want
any crybabies on my team.
Now, get Chacho to help you
untie these gloves 'cause you got 'em
on backward. When I blow
this here sporty gold whistle,

there's no turning back.
You listening?

"You hit the floor
with all you got, mister.
Just make sure
it's all in your gloves
and not in your pants."

Chacho's gonna get me in trouble
sooner or later. Can't believe it, yesterday, we stole
raisin pies from a Langendorf's bread truck on Treat Street.
Don't even like raisins.
Papi said, "I better never catch you stealing;
that's why your grandma Juanita
pulled your mother out of school in third grade."
All I've ever seen are apple and cherry pies,
like the ones at the restaurant counters when we got off at the
Greyhound bus rest stop on the way here, in Modesto. Papi
calls the Greyhound station *El Perro,* the hound. "Don't be a
chump!" Chacho said. "This is the Mission. Nobody cares."
So, I kneeled on the van's floor
and crawled into the back, but I bumped over a crate
of day-old pink French doughnuts.

Waiting
Waiting
Waiting
for Coach Egan.

When are you gonna
blow your stupid gold whistle?

Boom!
Boom!
Boom!
It's my heart
knocking against my bones.

UNIGÉNITO

"Whinnytoe!
Don't look at Sweet Pea when you're boxing!
He's got a glass eye. If you stare at it, it'll make you go nuts!"
Cadena laughs at me, then jabs Chacho in the ear.

Don't know what I am doing here.
"Boxing?" Mami says. "I never lika
you play those rough games.
No play with rough boys.
You get hurt. You are my *unigénito.*"

Mami says *unigénito* a lot.
The only one. The first and the last.
No brothers. No sisters. Well,
I almost had a sister — Andrea Dolores.

But Andrea Dolores died
when she was being born.
Sometimes when I think of my sister
something in my throat gets hard
and the *Idon'tknowwhat* is about
to sink into my chest.
Little hairs on my arms turn into pins
I get so tight and mad.
Hearts don't sink, do they?

"No rough stuff!
¡No andes peleando!"
Mami tells me looking up at me 'cause
I am so tall and she is so short. Then,
her eyes soften. "You are a handsome,
tall *muchacho.*"
She makes the sign of the cross
on my forehead. Mumbles sweet holy words.
I kiss her tiny hand when she's done.
That's how you show *respeto,* respect.
That's how I kissed my uncle Arturo's hand
when we arrived last week. We ate
at Foster's cafeteria, right across
from *El Perro* on 7th and Market Street.
Never been in a cafeteria.

Respeto, respect.
When I say it, my shoulders get soft.

Papi didn't come with us to San Francisco.
Said he was going back to El Mulato, Chihuahua,
his hometown,
to the *ojos de agua,* natural springs.
"Good for diabetes," he said.

Said he was going
to stay for a while. Said,

"I going to put thirty dollars down
on two acres for you, Son.
So one day, you'll have a *ranchito*."

Papi's always putting thirty dollars down
on a *ranchito* for me. He's got an ad from Kingston,
Arizona, in his cow-skin wallet that says:
"Cheap Land, $600 per acre."

We go here, go there. Move here,
move there. We're always going,
going, going. One of these days Papi's legs
are going to wear out. But
the *ranchito* never appears
for too long.

No rough stuff.
No rough stuff.
So, Mami buys me comics.
She tells me to repeat after her
the names of the saints
on the calendar in the kitchen.

Or Mami says,
Paciencia, paciencia. So,
I sit on the sofa and read

Superman and how he uses his special
powers to save the world.

Paciencia in
English is *patience.*
Sounds like "patients,"
grumpy bloody people in hospitals.

Cousin Chacho isn't patient.
Chumps are patient.

"Whinnytooooo!"

Coach Egan's whistle shakes me up.
Boom-Boom-Boom!
A bell goes off in my head.
It hurts and makes my eyes water.
It's 7:00 P.M. Sharp. The clock
behind the basketball hoop
glows hot and steamy and
sparkles mean.

Sweet Pea rises.

ask me about kryptonite

At the sharp edge of the ring
against the dirty ropes,
a bead of sweat rolls down my cheek.
Hope Coach Egan doesn't think it's a tear.

Sweet Pea snaps his gloves together like he's some
Sugar Ray Robinson, the welterweight champ
who is on a poster on our
bunk beds back on Harrison Street.

Boom!
Boom!

My shorts are goofy
with yellow and green stripes.
Look like a banana.

Boom!

Boom!

On the same wall,
there's a poster of Kid Dynamite,

a Mexican flyweight boxer from Tijuana.
That's just a few miles south from San Diego,
and another few
from Ramona Mountain.
Maybe I can be like him. But I'm not even really
from Ramona Mountain.

Boom!

Boom!

We just moved there 'cause
Papi's always thirsty, always dreaming things.
Before that Papi worked the tractor
on Mr. Weed's turkey farm east of Ramona Mountain.
We stayed there a few months.
That was the first house we lived in.

Sweet Pea slips slow from his corner.
His eyes burn. He crouches.

Before that, we moved from
crop to crop, Papi picking grapes,
Mami slicing and drying peaches,
in Fresno, Selma, Huron, and Dinuba.

Sweet Pea rises, floats and dances; he twirls
and rat-tat-tat taps his blue sleek gloves
against his forehead and sharp nose.
Wiry Sugar Ray
lollipop hammer fists.

"Go, *Primo!*
Andale!
That's my big bad cousin!" Chacho yells.
"Spank Sweet Pea good!"

We used to drive in Papi's old
chile-shaped Army truck
before he sold it to Mr. Weed for seventy dollars
so we could move to the other side of Ramona Mountain
where we stayed at Ranchito Garcia
and helped Mr. Garcia take care of his land.

Then, one day the green van came
like a monster from a deep lagoon.
Everything changed. That's why we are here.

Boom-Boom!
Boom-Boom!

Shudda told Chacho I don't fight.
Papi said, 'Talk to me first,'

but he's not here; he's never here.
He's walking around somewhere,
with a bucket in his hand, searching
for water.

Fight? Me?
Don't know how. Ask me
about Superman. Ask me about Kryptonite.
Shudda stayed in the bunk bed, on Harrison Street,
drawing my cartoons and watching TV.
Never had a TV before. Watch the Marx Brothers
where Harpo makes the face of a lighthouse,
looks like he's electrocuted and gamma rays
are shooting out of his mouth.
But he isn't really a lighthouse.
And Chacho's place
isn't really my house.

Don't even know if
Papi will come back
in a month or a year. He never says.
Mami doesn't tell me.

So I said, "Ok,
Chacho." I said, "Ok, ok,

Give me
the gloves.

"Give them
to me!"

I take two flabby steps
over the white mat.

MOrGUE rUN

July 1958

"Whinnytoe didn't wash his hands, Mom!"
Chacho sings out to Aunt Albina.

"Yes I did! My name is Juanito!"
I say, and rub my hands on my pants.
Stick out my tongue at him through a tortilla hole.

Mami shakes her head
rinsing the dishes and gazes over the refrigerator. Wonder
if she's looking at Granpa Alejo and Grandma
Juanita peeping down at me from their yellowish
oval photograph on the wall next to a chalky statue
of La Virgen de Guadalupe. We have the same photo
in Mami's jute bag. Mami says, "When we have our *ranchito*
I'll put the photographs of your *papa grande* and
your *mama grande* on the wall, too." *When?* I say
to myself.

"Soy la cafetera de la Harrison!"
I am the Coffee Queen of Harrison Street!
Aunt Albina blurts out, and slaps a coffeepot
on the table, laughs out loud, and swishes through
the pages of *Life* magazine.

The oval faces
over the refrigerator
make me feel like maybe things are slowing down,
like the way they used to be
when we lived at Ranchito Garcia
in our *traila* parked next to
the bell peppers and the pigs,
our homemade trailer Papi
made out of old wood slats
and a beat-up car chassis he found half-buried
on the outskirts of Escondido.

"Your grandpa Alejo had a *pulquería* in 1910.
Those were the days of Pancho Villa.
We lived in an old *barrio* in Mexico City
called *El Niño Perdido*. I was barely one year old
when he died," Mami would say.
"He was only forty years old."

"Why did he die, Mami?"
"He was very tired, Juanito.
Very tired."

Then, Mami would brush my hair back
gently and sing a *canción,* her favorite song,
Adios, mi chaparrita
Que ya se va tu Pancho
Mas allá del rancho
Y muy pronto volverá. . . .

Good-bye, my little one
Your Pancho is leaving
Going away from the rancho
One day soon he will return. . . .

I think of Papi
when Mami sings that song.

Where is he?
When will he come home?

THE FLYING
JALAPEÑO COUSINS

Saturday mornings on Harrison Street
we listen to Uncle Arturo's radio show
El Vocero del la Gente on 94-something AM.
He tapes the show in *El Hi-Fi Room,*
in his old shack outside the kitchen — a few
feet from Chacha's stinky
old rug-patch doghouse.

"Hey, Whinnytoe!"

Chacho makes monkey faces, hides behind Tito.
Smacks his lips. Gurgles his milk out backward
through two straws.

Alvinita, a sixth grader and my favorite cousin,
whispers, "Ignore him," works on her
insects assignment. She wears pink pedal-pushers and
smells like a strawberry shake. Then, Rosita,
the tiniest, just stands at the end of the table
with her dress puffed out like a Christmas tree.
Julie, Judy, and Gracie sit together,
comb their hair. They go to Mission High School,
giggle a lot.

The breakfast table is a wavy city
spread with towers of juicy beans,
two skyscrapers of Christopher's Milk in tall quarts,
a bank-basket of tortillas and a lake of salt in a plate.
You can pinch the salt and sprinkle it over
a hot buttered flour tortilla. Never had breakfast
like this. I roll a tortilla into a flute,
puff-puff out the steam, and
dip it into the red-juice beans.

"Hey, Pencil Neck!
Let's go one round!"

Chacho leaps up behind me.
Boom! My head jerks back,
his arm squeezing my neck.
I turn and swing as hard as a demolition ball,
but instead of hitting Chacho
I knock my milk into Mami's beans,
and flip the stack of tortillas into the air.

Flop,
Flap-flip,
Flop-splat!

I bump into Aunt Albina,
make her juggle a handful of jalapeños

so they fly up higher and higher and
rain down on the floor.

Pling!
Ploop!
Plap!
Plak-pluff!

Aunt Albina grabs both of us by the ears.
"Listen, *malcriados!*
You mess-ups are going to deliver
tortillas all day next Saturday.
No movies at El Capitan!"
Aunt Albina makes us
scoop up the green chiles
from under the table.

"Chump!" Chacho whispers, his elbow jabbing my ribs.

Chacho's making the hair
on my arms get stiff. One more
word from him and I am going
to sock him in the nose.
But,
I don't want to fight.
Papi said.

TECHNIQUE

"*Ya déjalo!*
Like, leave him alone, Chacho!"
big cousin Tito says, and pulls me aside.
His hair is combed into flappy sailboat waves
coiling down between his eyebrows.

"Like, don't let Chacho make fun of you, man.
Like, he's probably mad, 'cause I told him
to clean up Chacha's poop this week."

Cousin Tito pops a bean
into Chacho's glass of milk.
Swoosh-zap-splash!
"Like, see, Juanito, like all you need
is a little technique, Daddy-o.
Then, you'll be a hepcat, cool?"

"Ah . . . Chachoo!
Ah . . . Chachoo!"

Big cousin Tito
pretends he's sneezing,
but he's really making fun of Chacho.

"I bet neither of you cats
can do the 'Morgue Run.' Are you squares
or are you cool Daddy-os?"

"Run the uh, uh, what?"
I ask Cousin Alvinita, who
copies down a song that Julie's
singing to her.

My eyes are dim
I cannot see
I do not have
My specs with me. . . .

"Well, let me tell you," Alvinita
says, poking her front teeth with a pencil.
"This what *they say* they do, Juanito.
First you sneak up, and on your stomach,

crawl into a secret ventilator at General
Hospital, so you can see guys in white coats
pull out dead people's bloody guts in
the Autopsy Room where they pile up the intestines
on top of their gashed-open stomachs!
Livers like blue larvae. Ugh! Second,
with a bean shooter you spit out
little hard spitballs and see
if you can land them
inside the dead body. And, third,
when they go *locos* trying
to find you, you squeeze out, fast, like ketchup —
and this is the worst part — you race to the Freezer Room,
open one of the lockers, pull a bloody body out,
and let it bounce on the linoleum floor! Then you run, run!
All the way home."

Alvinita makes a face like
she just drank a sour lemon, rotten egg, and roach malt.

"Cool Daddy-o!"
Tito strokes his invisible goatee. "Cool!"

TING-TANG-TING

From the top of big Cousin Tito's drawer
on his twelve-transistor radio,
a song by Pedro Infante,
"Amor, Amor, Amor."

I think of Papi, somewhere
in the desert in Chihuahua, swimming
in an *ojo de agua.* Why doesn't he write?
Radio congas pop —
Bop-da-bop-plak!
Bop-plak-da-bop!

Everyone's chattering, laughing, jumping,
and slapping each other on the shoulder.
In the hallway, someone slides down
the curly stair banisters
and bounces out to Harrison Street.

Bop-
da-bop-plak!
Bop-plak-
da-bop!

Everything's too loud.
I plug my ears. Think of little rivers

of rain wearing their cloud hats,
rolling by our trailer in Ranchito
Garcia. When you touch them,
the hats disappear.

Switch on
Tito's red lightbulb lamp.
Makes the room
soft with watermelon colors —
watermelon pillows,
watermelon floor.

Lay down
on the watermelon bunk bed,
fold my arms over my watermelon chest,
my head against the watermelon wall.
So still — breathe on my watermelon hands
to make sure I am here.
Red, red, red.

Open up the toolbox Papi gave me.
Never noticed how scratched
and small it is. One tin soldier
is missing an arm, another a leg.

Where are you, Papi?
Why don't you send a postcard?

Bow my head, shoot
my cat's-eyes across the watermelon blankets.
Ting-ting — do the Morgue Run?

Gotta be a morgue runner.
Gonna run it all by myself. Faster
than a Greyhound, faster than Superman.
Gonna do the Morgue Run;
if I don't . . .
I might as well run all the way back home,
if I had one.

Ting-ting.
Ting-tang-ting.

THE TORTILLA DRAGON

Early every morning,
I help Aunt Albina pack sandwiches
in her deli, La Reina Mexicatessen,
on the corner of 20th and Harrison Street.
She sells *tortas,* tacos, sandwiches,
French rolls, Ibarra Chocolate, candies, sodas,
Christopher's Milk, and Orangeade. If you open

the door in the back of the deli,
you are in Uncle Arturo's Tortilla Dragon.
I call it the Tortilla Dragon 'cause it's a hissing machine.
With open chain jaws, it jerks and spins buzzing
pulleys that go kriii, kriii, kriii,
and sucks little balls of corn dough
from a shiny blob of crumbly, pasty corn mix
stuffed into a steel cone, spits them out
onto gray wire nets like roller-coaster tracks,
flattens and cooks the soft skins
on a spinning hot plate, and flings them
across the room.

They hit little Rosita on the face
when she tries to catch them.
She stacks them in a cardboard box.

Ready for delivery
in the Mission District.

Uncle Arturo says, "Juanito,
did you know that this is
the first tortilla-making machine
in the Mission? Everybody eats tortillas!"
Uncle Arturo slaps his apron, and a wobbly
cloud of flour floats over his face.

"Aunt Albina?" I ask.
"Can I go to El Capitan with Chacho today?
They're showing *The Monster from the Black Lagoon.*
And it only costs —"

Aunt Albina finishes what I am about to say,
"Two 7UP bottle caps and a dime!
But you *malcriados* drink *my* 7UPs!"

"Gonna do the Morgue Run by myself,"
I mumble, slide out the door.
Race down Harrison,
watch my feet disappear and
reappear under me. Run-run four long blocks,
run so fast my liver hurts — is the liver on
your right side or left side?

CrOW In THE FOrEST

Cars with wild flashy fenders melt colors
like turquoise and lipstick orange when the
lights change. Little girls skip on the white line
with *pan dulce* pop-popping laughter.
The sky,
never seen a sky like this,

rain blue at the center
with shredded clouds like leaves on a sky-tree.
I imagine each cloud leaf falling over the city.

Hey, little cloud, help me
find my way to the hospital and back home,
ok, ok?

In Ramona Mountain,
there is a forest.

When we had just moved from our first house
at Mr. Weed's turkey ranch, I smashed a five-gallon
glass bottle of spring water. I was trying
to pour it into the drinking jug. At Ranchito

Garcia all we had was a quart of water in a clay pot
Mami put outside at night so it would get cold.
Picking up the slivers of shattered glass
from the kitchen floor, Papi said,
"Water is life, Son!
It can heal you!
Now you take this empty bucket
and walk through the forest until you get to town.
And when you get there, find a way, a faucet,
fill the bucket with water. Bring it back full. Maybe, then
you'll learn how precious water is!"

The forest was dark;
each tree was a flame.

Each flame had a pair of eyes
that followed me. I could barely
see the sky. There was a tree
turned over by the side of the road
burned and broken in half;
under the skin its heart was red, yellow,
and still alive. I could tell
because it was soft and wet.
And there was a crow
standing on one of its broken limbs.

"Caw-caw-caw,
Juanito! Caw, caw!"
It seemed to say, "Help, help,
help!" Or maybe it said,
"Turn back, turn back,
or you won't find your way home!"

COUSIN ALVINITA'S
SECRET MAP

Cross Potrero, make a left.
   Walk for about half a block, then
climb the fence. Go over the big rock
   that looks like it has the Virgin Mary
carved into it. There's a wishing fountain
   under it. Cross the asphalt court
   where the cars park and run to the second
building made out of bricks. Kneel down
   on the curb and open the ventilator shaft.
It has a sign that says,

Do Not Open

   Crawl inside for about five feet and pull down
a vent window just a little so they won't
   see you and wait — don't make any noise
or try to get up 'cause you'll get stuck like a pig. Then wait —
   wait, for a body.

P.S. I wouldn't do it if I were you, Juanito.
   Your prima, Alvinita

inside the ventilator

Inside the ventilator,
everything's gray.
Scraped
my knuckles raw.

My Levi's, ripped at the knees, slimy
from the worms and snails and leaves that line the screens.
Smells like alcohol and oatmeal. Wait a minute;
someone's coming into the Operating Room.
She's washing her hands
and slippin' on a pair of orange gloves. She's pulling out a tray
of little hammers and saws, long silver pliers,
and a box of needles
and rubber coils. What's she gonna do?

A table on wheels rolls in
covered with something under a white blanket.
Looks like a bumpy *zarape*
with two long French bread rolls at the end.
Are those the legs?
Now a man walks in and uncovers the body.
Black-blue, orange, red, and
even green cloudy swirls cover the skin.
Looks like a tub of water,
like the one Mami uses to

wash all our clothes on Harrison Street.
A tub filled with dirty rags. Some knotted
into a head with flat buttons for eyes,
a shirt balled up into a stomach with
its orange pockets ripped open,
a pair of stiff pants with curly coffee stains for feet.
Where is the heart?

Where-where?

"Whinnytoo?"

Someone's tugging at my feet;
they pull-pull so fast I pop-scrape my lips
on the steely bottom of the ventilator.

"Why didn't you tell me
you were gonna do the Morgue Run?"
Chacho says with his eyes getting about as small
as two red ants from Ranchito Garcia.

"I, uh, was, uh . . ."
My lower lip swells.
I feel the salty scratch with my tongue.

"This is Edda, seventh grader at Everette!"
He points to a lanky guy with springy
yellow hair, freckles, and a sailor cap.
"The Morgue Run is for chumps!" Edda says
in a raspy voice.

"You need to stick with me, *Primo*,"
Chacho says, grinning from ear to ear.

"*This* is cooler than the old Morgue Run!"
Edda says pulling out a piece of chalk
from his pocket. He draws a curvy line on the sidewalk.
"We go from here, to there," he says, "then, to here!"
He draws a skull at the end of the line and writes

BIG DUKE'S
BAR

Edda hands me two beer bottles, and points.
"Head down Potrero to 20th Street; come on!"
"Wait!" says Chacho, pulling out
a jagged purple Lindy ink pen from his back pocket.
"First you gotta get the Harrison Street boy tattoo."
"The Harris —?"

"Shad-up and watch!"
he says with his mouth screwed to the side.

"Drop by drop
we stay on top . . ."
He pecks the sharp point of the pen
onto the top of my hand.

"Say it!" he says. . . .
"Drop by drop
we stay on top. . . .

Break the clock,
make it stop. . . .

Drop by drop
we stay on top. . . ."

A purple triangle
with an

HS

in the middle.

It is a jet,
a knife, a torn leaf,
a piece broken off from a distant star.

"Now spit on it," Edda says.
"Now slap it!" Chacho says.
He slams me on the shoulder, then
Edda takes two shots.

Bam-blam!
Blam-bam-blam!

"Next time, you better beat Sweet Pea,"
Chacho says through his teeth.

The pain inside my shoulder is a spider.
It crawls over my arm down to my hand.
Hot water wells up in my eyes.
"Don't rub it! 'Cause, then you're out!"
Chacho says, and grins.

"Run! Run!"
Edda's throaty voice rumbles.

Make a right and keep on flying until
we reach Big Duke's on Alabama.
Chacho opens the blond wooden doors
and launches his beer bottle inside.
Edda steps up and hurls his.
Swoop! Swoop!

"Your turn."
Chacho smiles sneaky. "Mountain boy!"

Raise the bottle high up
with my left hand, can't see anything
in front of me or all around, can't tell
if I'm still in the ventilator or waiting
in line at *El Perro*, waiting for a door to open,

climb on a bus, find a seat, stare at the black
waves ahead.

Papi, you said, "Don't get in trouble," but
this isn't trouble, is it?

Whooosh!

ENSIMISMADO

"I told you more than once, Juanito,
No play rough. But you don't listen to me.
I don't know what is happening to you.
Ever since we came to San Pancho, you don't talk,
you don't listen! If your papi was here,
he would say,

'You are all wrapped up in yourself!'
Ensimismado —
that's what you are, inside-yourself,
full of yourself. Look at you. You lip is broken,
your face, little cuts. Your pants are torn.
This morning a policeman came to the house and
asked questions about three boys.
What were you doing yesterday, Juanito?"

"Mami," I say and then stop.
I want to cry into Mami's hair
and have her hold me tight,
tell me everything is okay,
but I am a Harrison Street boy now.
I touch my hand, the triangle with *HS*.

"Look, Juanito,
if you keep getting into trouble,

we are going to have to move. Okeh?
We'll get a little apartment. And you'll go
to another school, where you won't see these *locos* again.

"Not talking, eh?"

"I have a sore tooth, Mama," I mumble.
"Maybe I should stay home from school this week?"

"Well, we'll see. . . . You know,
if you lie to your mother,
that is enough to ruin the rest of your life and your soul
will rot and end up wandering in Purgatory when you die.
Then you will see me standing there in front of you!
Look at me," she says in her scary Halloween voice.
She rolls her eyes up, like she's dead.
"So, no more play rough, eh? Your papi said, eh?
I am not going to ask you anymore. Come on;
maybe we need to go out and get some fresh air.
When we lived in Juárez . . ."

Mami tells me her story for the hundredth time.

"When I was a young woman,
I had the best job at El Camino Restaurant in El Paso
on Paisano Drive. My hair was thick and auburn —
do you know what auburn is, Juanito?"

"Uh-burn?"

"Auburn,
castaño — starry brown-red. I had long auburn hair
and the wind would blow it across my face and
shoulders. The air was so fresh it was as if it was filled with
tiny snow flakes and tickly leaves of sunlight.
We lived in Juárez in the thirties —
that's when Mama Grande Juanita was still alive.

"Then one windy afternoon, in the autumn of 1940,
she died of a stroke, right in the kitchen.
My dear mama. I had taken care of her
since I was a teenager. That was my
duty as the youngest daughter. I don't want
you to do that for me. I want you to be free."

My mouth is shut.
I want to tell her about everything, about
stealing pies and throwing bottles and
the green van and . . .

But things are too big to talk about, and
I can't even say one word.
What would she say?

divurssho

We visit Uncle Lalo and Aunt Faustina
on 16th and Mission Street
when the well-fair check comes in
at the beginning of the month. Uncle Lalo always
has things for sale that he buys at the
pawnshops on Howard Street.

Uncle Lalo makes fun of Papi because
Papi doesn't pronounce words like he does.
"I know about words," he always tells me.
"I was going to be a lawyer in Mexico City but
couldn't afford to go to school, so I sold clothes
in Barrio Tepito, saved money, married your *tía* Faustina,
wore a hat and a tailor-made cashmere suit,
came to the U.S. to work in laundry. Every day
I practiced English reading the tags on the shirts!"

Uncle Lalo's always talking about being somebody
or about building a house that he never lives in.
Every time we visit him and Tía Faustina on Mission Street,
he says to Mami, "Gonna build a house in Atizapán, Lucha,
a few miles north of Mexico City, see these *fotos?*
That's the bathroom; Faustina loves blue tile, the balcony."

But Uncle Lalo never leaves; he just
scribbles plans in little books that pile up in his closet.
Once Uncle Lalo starts he never stops talking.

"*Di-vor-ci-o,* not *divurssho!*
Divor-cio! Not *divurrsho!*

"Your father can't even say *divorce* right," he tells me.
"You know what he told your mother, don't you?
He said that if she doesn't like how he lives
and how he likes to go to those so-called
healing springs, then she can get a *divurrsho!*
He can't even say it right! Are you listening, Juanito?"
Uncle Lalo pokes me in the forehead with his stubby finger.

Sit down next to Mami.
Quiet. Everyone quiet.

All I hear is my heart,
then, the cartoon music.

THE HARRISON
STREET KING

August 1958

ELECTRIC YELLOW
SUNLIGHT ON 20TH

Cars in yellow sunlight,
buses in cloud colors,
a fire truck in a glassy candy apple cape,
buildings like wrinkled accordions all in a row —
some stand to one side, soft and powdery,
as if they were made out of colored chalk.
Wires! So many wires.
Wires into wires into wires connecting everything
so buses can drive through the streets — electric.

Everything is electric — the streets during the day
and at night, in rainbow dresses and neon parade hats.

Chacho stops outside Big Duke's Bar.
Takes a dead mouse out of his front pocket.
"Trade you for your Duncan yo-yo? How about
that prehistoric rock?" he says, pointing.
I take out a wrinkled stone
I found at Potrero Hill,
in the shape of a lopsided heart.

"Just kidding," he says, and slaps me in the shoulder.
"Race you to my house," he says, running ahead of me.

Mami said,
"You visit your cousins, but come home early.
Don't get lost. Remember, now we live at
Twenty forty-four Mission Street, number two. Second floor.
No more getting in trouble
with those *locos* on Harrison Street!"

At least we didn't move to another town.
Maybe we should have — Aunt Faustina
and Uncle Lalo live two inches from
our apartment. We're in #2;
they're in #3.

When I threw those bottles into Big Duke's Bar
thought I saw Papi sitting there.
See him everywhere. Rub my eyes.
At Patrick Henry Elementary, my new school,
sometimes it looks like he's standing
under the black clock by the door,
waiting for me, wearing his straw white hat
and his favorite blue coat. If he was here
Mami wouldn't have to work so hard.
If we were in Ramona Mountain and if Papi
still had his big-nosed Army truck
we would be driving into Ranchito Garcia,
parking in the shade of an avocado tree.
But he's not here.

And we are not there.
Papi's somewhere
in Mexico or New Mexico —
I forget which Mexico —
looking for water that will cure him.
Why does he need water?
What's wrong with him?

Uncle Lalo thinks Papi is crazy. Aunt Faustina thinks
he's too old and doesn't know how to live in the big city
because Papi speaks only a little and when he does —
like when Uncle Lalo was making Mami buy me
one of his old pair of shoes for six dollars —
Papi says things like,
"Get the hecka outta here!"

"How did Uncle Lalo get a hunchback?" I ask Mami.
"Be kind," Mami says. "Always.
It's all the work he's done, bowing down
into laundry tubs." I don't say it but I think he got it
by dragging home all the crooked machines
he buys on Howard Street.
There are winding machines he keeps
stacked on the kitchen floor,
talking machines with numbers and glass fuses he sells, and
round TV-screen machines with electric submarine sounds
that he plans to take to his new house in Mexico.

"Your uncle wanted to be a lawyer," Mami tells me.
"He had dreams. But the only things
he works with are hot boiling rags
and stinging steam engines
that go round and round and round
and never get anywhere.
You understand?"

double lucky

Cousin Alvinita, who's a year older than me,
dribbles the basketball next to the fire hydrant.
"How come you haven't come by, Juanito?
You haven't even come to catechism on Saturdays!"
She shoots the ball to me, smiling.

I shoot the ball back to her and miss.
"I am traffic safety now at Bryant School.
Too bad you changed schools," she says
hugging the ball, looking at me
with her big almond-shaped eyes and
long gold-brown silky hair, almost to her knees.

"What about the Duncan!" Chacho says,
shooting the ball to my chest.
I drop it and watch it roll into the street.

My yo-yo still smells new, like grape Popsicles, like Kool-Aid,
and Cousin Tito taught me
four yo-yo tricks.
The Cradle.
Walking the Dog.
Over the Bridge.
Around the World.

"All right. . . ."
I shrug my shoulders
and toss Chacho my rain blue yo-yo.

"This is a double lucky rat," he says.
"But if you don't take care of it,
you'll get double loads of rotten bad luck!"

Harrison Boy

Pass El Faro Taquería,
singing Alvina's and Julie's song.
My eyes are dim
I cannot see
I do not have
My specs with me . . .

Riiing!
Criiing! Griiing!
Sounds like a metal snowflake.
By the trash can
something sparkles. So small. What is it?
I kick again.
Riiing! Criiing! Griiing!

A gold ring?
With a blue stone that shines
as if it was carrying the ocean in a tiny window of glass.
Are these diamonds? Count them. One, two, three, four,
five, six, seven. . . .
Put it on. *Perfecto.*
Just wait till I show Chacho and Edda.

Pass Chi-chi's Nite Club,
make a fast right onto Mission and 20th.

Oh no! There's Mami.
She's going inside Ziggy's Pawn Shop.
It's gotta be her, because she's wearing her black winter coat
and her Dick Tracy dark sunglasses. "I wear them," she says,
"so people won't stare at me. People here
always stare. Do they think I have two heads?"

I know what she's thinking —
I am going to put these rings to work.
That's what Mami always says at the end of the month.
Papi brought her a gold band from Chihuahua last year.
And Tito gave her a cool cat ring he won
at a cable car ringing contest. "It doesn't fit
my bongo hands," he said.

Not going to tell her about my ring.
She'll put it to work, too.

I turn away, toward El Capitan Theater, keep walking
past the Doggy Dinner, The Town Pump Bar,
cross Yee's Produce with his boxes of mangoes, oranges, apples,
cucumbers, and short, stubby pink-purple bananas.
Sneak by Lochman's Furniture Shop
and I am home — 2044 Mission Street,
right next to Gayle's Fashions.

Walk up to the door. Pull at my keys
Mami pinned into my pocket.

Press my face against the window.
Is this where I live?
On the second floor?

First, you pass
the shower room with the yellow plastic curtain,
the toilet room, then, at the end
of the hall, our door — the one the left, #2.
Across from us is #3.
Uncle Lalo and Aunt Faustina's place
smells like mothballs.
Aunt Faustina stuffs them in her doll collection.
"Don't break the dolls," Mami says. "They belonged
to Aunt Faustina's daughter, Amelia."
One day while she was playing kickball
on Natoma Street, Amelia fell
back on her head and never opened
her eyes again. Sometimes
I think Aunt Faustina is mean to Mami because
Mami has me.

The stairs are dark.
Climb, climb in slow, spongy steps.
Unlock the brown door.
Turn on the lamp.
Slip my new ring on. Lay
the little lucky dead rat on the bed.

Sit in Mami's smooth black chair.
Rock myself
in the silent room, like a king,
a Harrison Street king.

What happened to the sleepy animals in Ramona Mountain?
What happened to the tadpoles that swished
in muddy puddles?
What happened to the fiery rooster
that chased me across the onion patch?

MERCUROCHROME IS
THE COLOR OF FIRE

Mami's next door
helping Tia Faustina with the dishes.
I told them I had homework.
"Got homework," I said. "*Tengo* homework,
on the Incas, for Mr. Heyden's class."

My new school is Patrick Henry Middle School by
Potrero Hill.
Gotta catch a bus at Marshall Elementary.
Marshall only goes to high fourth. I am in low fifth.
I go with Georgey Wong, Rudy Maldonado,
Sylvia Trujillo, James Quentin Reesgo,
and Becky Melendez.

After Mami saw my Harrison Street tattoo
on my left hand
she said, "No more Boys Club with those *locos* — ever again!"
Then she gave me fifty cents.
"I put my rings to work." She smiled
and shut the door.

I haven't shown her my ring.
She won't believe me. She'll say "those *locos*" stole it.
Then, she'll take it and put it in a little jar with her buttons

and wait a couple of months until it's Christmas.
Take it to the pawnshop. Make it work for us.

I mix alcohol and
Mercurochrome inside a milk glass.
Then I suck it up with a dropper
and put a few drops into my lucky rat's mouth
so he won't stink.
Hang him by the tail by the window
with one of Mami's wooden clothespins.
Oh no!

His tail snaps off; there he goes
down a narrow crevice
between our building and Gayle's Fashions.
I can see him. A tiny busted gray spot.
"I am sorry, Lil' Lucky," I say softly.

Pump the red-orange liquid
into an electric socket behind the front door.
Pretend I am a doctor.
I am healing the house. So I'll be lucky and Mami, too.
So all my friends can come and visit,
so maybe Papi can come home, too, so
Mami won't have to light candles at night
asking the Virgin Mary
questions about Papi —

Can you make him return safely to us?
Can you make him happy to be in one place?
Make him stop running around like a gypsy.

Shoot more red-orange milk
into the two thin plastic lips
on the wall, next to the lamp.
Nothing — then,

Whoosh!
Whoosh!

A tongue of fire spits out of the black holes,
puffs out a ball of gray smoke, melts the socket
into gray metal gravy — the lamplight
goes out. Poof! Poof!

More fire.
More smoke.
More gray gooey plastic metal gravy.
A weird alarm goes off.
Blaang! Blaang! Blaaang!
Sparks fizzle out from the wall.

Mami comes in, bats the air
with a dish-washing towel.

"*Que estas haciendo!* What on earth are you doing
in the dark?"

"A rat tried to crawl into the socket, Mami.
You should have seen it. His head was on fire.
He was dancing on the floor, like a little *mariachi*!
Then he ran into the kitchen and
leaped out the window and committed suicide!"

Mami walks over
and peers at Lil' Lucky.
"Ay! I wish Felipe was here," she says, rubbing one eyebrow.
Walks stiff and slow down the hall to the manager's place,
Apartment #1. Mrs. Nishkan, who has hair like
a licorice ladder.
A long warty nose like a circus pickle.

Sit down on the bed
in the gray room.
Feel the scabby, scraggly Harrison Street tattoo.
It's the only way I know I am here and
not there, floating from one spot
to another in the smoky dark.

Mami says I can't visit
Harrison Street for a week. "That's where you
get all those *ratas* and bad ideas in your *cabeza!*"
"It's ok. It's ok," I say.

Instead, I go to the rock on Potrero Hill
in the shape of a doll. Chacho showed me.
A few flowers at her feet.
She's looking down from the top of the boulder,
a little teardrop-shaped face with gray-white eyes,
her arms reaching out, as if
inviting me to come in. From far away
she looks like a soft wing growing out of the hill.

"Are you thirsty?" I ask her. "What's your name?
My name," I tell her, "is Juanito Palomares.

"How old are you?" I say, cleaning leaves
from her shoulders. "I bet you are
seven. I am ten. See my card? Do you have
a Boys Club card?
I mean a Girls Club card?
Mine is white with my name in red type.
Be careful, ok? There's a spider right

behind you. I'll hit it with a rock, ok?
You didn't tell me your name.
Dee LaRosa?

"Do you like that name?
Dee LaRosa? Sounds like raindrops,
like the tiny flower on your dress,
like the name of a girl in my class —
Ana de LaRosa. Shhh.
Don't tell anybody.
She's pretty with long bouncy black hair
and freckles and cherry red lips.
She sits in the front row.

"Yesterday, Mr. Heyden
asked us why the Incas dressed with gold
and she said, 'Because they loved the sun
and the sky and painted themselves
with the colors of the heavens.'
I think she's a poet.

"See my new ring?
Made of gold, a sapphire,
and seven diamonds?
And look at this!" I show Dee LaRosa my scratched *HS*.
"Even better, huh?

I better go, Dee LaRosa."
Cross the street in yellow sunlight.
Buses in misty colors. A fire truck roars down
20th Street toward the Regal Pale Brewery.

"Bye."

HOUSE EMPTY

Mexico feels like a house
where we used to live
so long ago no one remembers it
or knows exactly where it is.

We always seem to talk about it though.
Papi goes back and looks for it,
but I don't think he's found it yet. Mami says
he knows where he's going
but I think he's lost
and doesn't know where the house
is anymore; he circles it.
Loses it again.
Why can't this be Mexico?

Maybe that's why Papi looks for water.
Water that will cure him. So he can feel at home.

STINKY BAIT

"You like fish, huh?"
Georgey Wong asks me
in the Patrick Henry School cafeteria.
I usually bring a baloni sandwich
or a potato burrito, but this morning
Mami gave me money to buy
a tuna fish sandwich from Bonami's Market.

Cafeteria is the same in Spanish — café-tería.
When I pronounce the words in Spanish,
I remember them. When I don't, they're hard
to remember. They get harder every day,
but I don't tell Mr. Heyden. If I tell him
he's gonna think I am dumb,
gonna say, "Why don't you know
all these words on your spelling list?
All the students in class know them,
except you!"

Mr. Heyden doesn't know that
every time we move, my spelling list
moves, too.

"Hey, Johnny!
You like fish? Are you deaf?"

Wong makes a Laurel and Hardy face
with his long chin,
his mouth screwed to one side.

"My name is Juanito!" I yell across
the table. "Not Johnny!" Georgey
makes a face like he just smelled
a dead cat crawling with ants.

People think he's my brother because
we're about the same color and wear
the same kind of checkered shirts and
have choppy butch haircuts and act goofy.

Moses Simpson sits across from us.
He's the toughest and smartest guy.
I am the tallest. Yesterday,
Mr. Heyden asked him, "Why
can't a chicken with cut wings fly
over the fence?" "Balance," smarty-pants Moses said.
Just one word — *balance.*

"You guys stink!"
Moses says, standing up from his bench.
"Get away!" Then he makes
the ugliest face in the world.

Gluey water runs down my nose.
Wipe it with my knuckles.
Georgey shoots me a wrinkled handkerchief.
"Your nose is bleeding like a donkey," he says.

Sit outside on a bench with Georgey and listen to him
sing and wiggle his head
to make me happy.

Peggy Sue
Peggy Sue
I love you
Peggy Sue . . .

The bell rings
from far away across
the yard. Moses and two boys
wait around the tetherball pole, stare
at me and Georgey. Then they blast off
running after us.
Moses chases me across the yard
in little circles and big circles.

I stop and turn around.
"Wanna box!" I say out loud.
"I belong to the Mission Branch Boys Club

Boxing Team! And we're mean!"
My nose half-wet, half-dry, red-runny.

Face Moses made of sunlight.
"What team?" Moses says.
"You're so dumb."

"Come on! I am
Kid Dynamite!" I say, and smile.

Moses stands before me with his fists
curled tight like combination locks.
"Wash your face, dummy!
Go crying back to your mama!"

Drop by drop
we stay on top!
Break the clock,
make it stop!
I want to start to cry a little
but nothing comes out,
like I have gravel eyes and
gravel eyelids.

Wipe my nose again, fast
so no one can tell.

MUHi pier

"Greetings!"
Georgey Wong says
outside Bonami Market
where we meet on Saturday, 7:00 A.M.
"Come on, we gotta catch the number fourteen.
And don't forget to ask for a transfer
when we get to Van Ness."

"Why do you always say, 'Greetings'?" I ask.
"Dunno," Georgey says.

We transfer and the bus
scoots up over Nob Hill,
then Chinatown.

"Want some spaghetti?"
Georgey says. The best spaghetti
is from Chinatown,
on Stockton Street,
not Grant or Columbus in North Beach
where all the tourists go!

The electric antennas
spark from the yellow-green bus
gripping the high wires

connecting us
to every house
except Ramona Mountain,
except Papi.

"Where's the pier?" I ask Georgey.
"Down there. At the end
of Van Ness Street.
Wait;
first we need bait."

We race over to the Bay Street Bait Shop.
"That's bait? Looks like sardines from Italy."
"It's bait. Just bait. Taste?"
Georgey swings a smelt over his nose.

He drops it.
"You drop it, you buy it!"
a man with a red wool vest says,
wiping the counter with a wet towel.
Georgey pays with a twenty-dollar bill.
"Precisely!" Georgey says in an English accent.

We both squeeze out of the door
at the same time. "Here, this
bait's for you." Georgey ties a

plastic bag of bait to my belt.
Ties another bag to a slinky chain on his.

"Want some money?"
Georgey asks. "I got it from my grandma's purse.
It's ok. She never goes out. She just sits at
home sweeping and talking about Chinatown.
In the morning she goes up on the roof,
does tai chi, and moves her hands across
the wind as if she is lifting giant balloons;
she calls each move a name, like Jade Maiden
Rousing the Monkey,
and Smoothing the Horse's Brain.
Or something like that.
Here's five dollars," he says, and pushes a crumbled
green star into my shirt pocket.

"Take it. I'll get more next week.
Let's go!"
We run down a block to the shore
and stop. The fog rolls under
the Golden Gate Bridge, blows
across the sky, and curls over the trees.

What will Mami say about the money?
She says that if I ever do anything bad
my soul will be lost in Purgatory. That if
I tell lies or steal or cheat or hit anyone
she will know.

"All I have to do is look at you.
Your eyes speak."

EYEBALLS FiLLED WiTH HONEY

"That's Alcatraz,"
Georgey points at a little island
in the middle of the bay. "That's a prison.
Nobody gets out of there. You'd have to swim
with the sharks," Georgey says, puffing
his chest. "And that bridge is the Golden Gate!
Like the color of salmon eggs.
Ever chewed salmon eggs? Like red eyeballs filled
with honey!"

"Where's the pier?"
I ask him. "Where?"

"You're standing on it!"
"This is the pier?" I say, looking at the concrete
tongue that curves out into the ocean.

Georgey knots the crab-net rope
to a concrete bench, opens the crab net,
a giant clam made out of wire.
"Give me some bait; hurry!"
I grab the smelt from my bag and
pass it to Georgey. He coils it into

a ball and locks it inside a small wire
box in the middle of the clam mouth.
"The crabs have little eyes,
but they can see good!"

"What will the crab say if it sees this?"
Show him my diamond ring.

"You got that at Woolworth's, huh?"
"No way!"
"Yes you did!"
"No, I didn't!"

"Here," Georgey says, and grabs it.
"Let's put it into the bait box so it will give us good luck."

"I bet you Mr. King Crab
will see my ring from miles away!"
I say, rubbing my hands. Georgey stuffs the ring
into the knotted slimy ball of smelt fish heads.

"Throw it into the water!
Before the tide goes down!
Hurry!

"If you don't hurry
all we're going to get is a dogfish
or we'll hit a snag and lose everything."
"What's a snag?"
"Gimme that."

Whoosh-shoosh-splish!

We sit on the bench for hours.

Flap our arms like seagulls,
talk about Mr. Heyden, and
Ana de LaRosa, who told Georgey
that she likes me.

The sun looks misty like a moon
with a cloud hat.

We stop at the end of the pier
and lean on the edge
where seagulls wait for handouts.
San Pancho looks like an island
made of soft white and powder blue
candle buildings. An island of fog
and silver lights.

"A pirate ship! Come on; let's go!"
I point across the pier.

"That's not a pirate's ship!
That's Fisherman's Wharf —
where tourists pay
a lot of money for crab and hot sauce."

We hunt our crab.
We're crab hunters!

"The tide!" he screams.
We run back to our bench.
"Crab! King Crab!" I yell.
"We got a crab!"
I dance around the bench.

"Let's see, ol' chap," Georgey says.
"Let's see. Mmmmm."
We both squat down and open the net
as if we were operating on a heart.

"This crab's yours. Ok. It's yours!
I'll get the next one," Georgey says,
stretching his shiny eyebrows.
He picks up the fuzzy brown crab. It opens
its spiny legs like a clock ticking
time in all directions. "Catch!"

I duck and the crab hits the concrete bench
and cracks its back. "Where's the ring?" I ask.
The crab's little shiny eyes move back and forth.

"Right there," Georgey points. "Hey,
ever had crab before?"
Georgey pets the shell.

"You have to boil it first.
When it turns red, it's ready."

I lay the crab down
and cover it with a towel.

The sun breaks into a thousand seashells on
the waves rolling in from *whoknowswhere*
rolling out to everywhere.
They come in on little boats, like half moons,
carved out of salty light.

Papi would love this ocean.
If he was here. Water is precious.

EL PERRO
MORNING SPECIAL

September 1958

ahijado party

Aunt Faustina says tonight is
going to be *"muy super-importante!"*

She says this dusting her little dolls
leaning up against each other.

"Tonight, we go to your uncle Arturo's house.
You better behave! And stop moving around
all the time, like a jumpy worm. Learn to be still.
My sister, Lucha, didn't know how to raise you.
With that father of yours,
out there in the wild winds, sleeping with chickens,
coyotes, and roosters! Tonight
you better behave. Mrs. Nishkan told me
that you set fire to the electric sockets
in your room. You almost burned down
the whole building! *Travieso!* You wildcat!

"Tonight, you'll see;
 you'll meet Armodio, my *ahijado*,
my godchild. Him and his mama are here visiting
from Atizapán de Zaragoza, Mexico.
That's the the birthplace of our president,
Adolfo Lopez Mateos. Do you know that?
What are you learning in school?

Never mind." Aunt Faustina clicks her tongue
and nods her head as if she's talking
to someone who will never know Mexico.

"Armodio, now, listen,
that's a well-behaved boy!" she says,
polishing a big doll made of pink clay.

Mami sits and winks at me while
Aunt Faustina has a conversation with herself.

"You want to wear one of my coats? Lucha?
They've seen you wear that black coat too many times.
They're going to think that is all you have, Lucha!
You're not in mourning, are you?
Well, you never know with that husband of yours."

Mami says, "It doesn't matter what color
the coat is — if you
wear red, people will criticize you and —"
"Okeh, okeh, I know, I know," Aunt Faustina says.
"But you don't have anything
that's red, do you? That's a color a decent
woman should never wear. It's a devil color."

"Ay, Faustina, why do you say all these things?
Why are you always so angry?" Mami says,

sitting quietly.
Aunt Faustina ignores her.

Maybe Aunt Faustina
is waiting for one of her dolls
to open her mouth and say a word,
like her daughter used to, before she died.

"Here, finish tying the apron on this one, Juanito!
So when Lalo comes home, everything will look
fresh and *elegante* like back home in Mexico, in Atizapán."
Aunt Faustina puts on her long coat —
from the Empoorium department store.
Aunt Faustina says "Empoorium."

We step out
into the early sharp blue night
on the streets.

THE MAGIC RAT IN THE BOX
AND A LONG HAIR

Armodio is almost as tall as me
and quiet.
Hair split down the middle,
one-half combed over one ear,
the other half over the other one.
Black shoes shiny like crows
and suspenders tight on his wide shoulders.
Warts on one side
of his face — like BBs.

Aunt Faustina pours Madero whiskey into a tiny glass
and drinks all of it as if
it is unwinding a ribbon of cool
honey down her throat. "Ahh! A toast!
For my *ahijado*, the smartest boy
and most handsome *caballero*," she says.

"He knows how to ride a horse.
He knows how to pray at church.
He knows how to sit still and he knows
how to speak Spanish properly and
he knows how to behave."

Aunt Albina pours herself
a mug of steaming black coffee.
"*Salúd!*" she says.
Mami applauds twice and then
folds her hands.

Tía Faustina says, "Now Armodio,
don't let Juanito and Chacho
drag you down Harrison Street."

Armodio shrugs his shoulders,
leans on the wall, and starts talking to Cousin Alvinita
who is tying Rosita's braids with a ribbon.
"My father owns a ranch in Mexico,"
he says, snapping his suspenders.
"And my horse is black, like a river at night.
His name is *Látigo*, whip. So fast,
he disappears. You like horses?"

"A horse?" she starts to say.
"Hey, Armonioo!" I call.

"Arrrrmodio!" he corrects me.
"Aren't you going to open your presents?" I ask him.
"Aunt Faustina says it's time to open them."

Aunt Faustina takes another long sip of Madero
and stands as if she's about to give a speech.
"Of coursh!" she says, walking sideways to us. "Lesh opinum. . . ."
Armodio tears the paper off of a square package.
"It's a little Bible?" he says in surprise.
"Like it? For church. . . ." Aunt Faustina says,
slipping a little to one side.
Then Armodio opens the orange bag
that Mami brought and pulls out
a ball-shaped package.
"What's this?" Armodio wrinkles his nose.
"Oopinut . . . ," Aunt Faustina insists.

It's a box with a circus rubber rat inside
like the one Mami and me saw on Market Street.

I take the box from Armodio and show
him how to paste the plastic hair to the bottom
of the rat and tie the other end to your belt.
"All you have to do is put the rat on your hand
and slide your hand away. See?
It's moving!" I say, "See! It's alive!
Just like a real one. I had one; it was a lucky rat!"
Armodio grabs it away and pops it
against the wall.

"Do you know how to ride a horse?
Do you know what *pulque* is?
Do you know how to collect *aguamiel?*
Do you know how to skin a pig?
You stink like rotten milk!
You're a *pocho,* aren't you?
You can't speak English right
and you can't speak Spanish right, huh?"

"Yes, I can!"
"No, tu no sabes nada!"
"Yes, I can!"
"Nada, de nada!"
"Yes, I . . ."

I run into Chacho and Tito's room
and pull out a pair of Chacho's old boxing gloves.
"Try this!"
I say to Armodio. "Armoodio?"
"Arrrmodio!" he says, and puts the gloves on.
Chacho rushes us into the watermelon room.

"I know how to box!"
"No you don't!"
"Yes I do!"

Armodio bobs his arms in front of his face,
with a grin.

"Ever hear of El Ratón Macías?"
he asks me.
"He's Mexico's boxing champion;
my father knows him. And he taught
me some tricks!"

"You know Sweet Pea Price?"
I ask Armodio.
"I didn't think you did."

"Ready?"
Chacho says.
"When I ring the bell,
you guys start!
Ready?
Come, on, Juanito.
You're big, so be big!"

"Ready!" I say.
"Listo, como látigo!" Armodio says,
smashing his gloves
against his chest.

Chacho rings the bell.

I throw a fast looping punch to Armodio's ear;
he ducks and shoots a fist into my belly. I double over
gasping for breath, but there is no air in the watermelon room.
Armodio bounces on his toes.

"Here's two more shots, you chump!"
Whoosh! Smash!

I miss again
and Armodio punches me in the nose. Boom!

Boom-boom-blam!
My glove flies off and
Whoosh! Blam! My fist comes back
with a double punch — bop-bop!
I cut Armodio's cheek.

He touches his face in the watermelon room.
Armodio opens his mouth,
but nothing comes out.

"I am sorry . . . ," I say,
"Uh, you can have my ring, ok?"
I pull out my gold ring from my pocket.
"It's a real sapphire and it's got six diamonds."
"I don't want your cheap ring!"

Chacho pulls me to one side.
"Whinnytoe! Don't give him your ring.
Are you a chump or a champ?"

Tía Faustina pops the door, grabs Armodio.
Brushes his hair back from his forehead.
Then she turns to me.
"You *tonto*, dummy, Juanito!
I warned you and Chacho!
Dame tu cinto! Give me your belt, Chacho!
Vas a ver, just wait!"

She looks at the belt and tries to stretch it.
"This isn't a belt, it's a piece of rope!"
She slaps it on the floor.
"Vas a ver," she says, "when we get home.
You're gonna learn."

"I can rip his head off!"
Armodio says, crying.
"Ish ok, my son," Tía Faustina says,
and trips out of the room.
"We're leaving," she yells out
to Mami. "Luchaa!"

"That was a solid left hook, Cousin,"
Chacho whispers. "Here's your ring.
And don't give your stuff away.
If it's yours it's yours and nobody else's."

Mami and Tía Faustina rush me out of the house
and walk me outside. They don't say anything.
Mami walks by my side.
Tía Faustina wobbles
on the corner of Tía Albina's Mexicatessen.
Under the cold wide-eyed lamp of the street.

"Wassamatterwit you, Juan!
Lucha, when are you going to teach him respect?"

I walk by Mami with my fists tight.
The streets look like stretched black cellophane
about to pop.
I wish Papi was here.
But he isn't.

"What happened when you got home last week?"
Chacho asks me at the Boys Club.
"Nothing. Well, Aunt Faustina doesn't talk to me or Mami
anymore. Well, she kinda does, but
we don't go to her apartment much.
Hey,
why do you have your shirt on backwards?"
I ask Chacho.

"It's not on backwards.
Yours is on backwards, Whinnytoe!"
"No way!" I say, thumbing the buttons
down to my stomach.
"Yes they are! And so are your pants!"
"No, *your* pants are on backwards!"
I tell him, and step back to take
a good look at him.
"You are all backwards!"

"No, *you* are, Whinnytoe!"
Coach Egan says, stepping into the front door.
His shirt is on backwards, too.

"It's Crazy Day at the Boys Club!
Didn't you know that?

On Crazy Day, we dress inside out and upside down.
And we put on our shoes on backwards
and watch movies and do skits.
Come in, but you gotta get crazy with your clothes!
Don't you get tired of being you all the time?"
Coach says, making a crooked grin.

I twist my clothes all around.
"The skit is about to start," Chacho says. "Sit down and watch."
What's a skit? I wonder.

"Ladies and gentlemen,
the Mission Branch Boys Club is proud to present
Los Crazyboys, directed by Coach Egan . . . and performed
by our very own boxing champs,"
Sweet Pea Price says with an inside-out sweater
and one red boot,
one green sock, on the other foot

"ACTION!"
Coach Egan shouts behind the curtains.

Then, I cough.
Kra-kraw!
"My backward collar is strangling me!"

I tell Chacho, who's telling me something
at the same time.

"Hey, are you listening?
My mom said
that your father's home!
And that you're leaving soon!"

daniel boone YELLOW

I run home from the Boys Club,
fly up the stairs, and pop open the door.

There is Papi in the tiny kitchen
drinking a tall glass of water.
"This water is almost as sweet
as the water in Tulare, where
the bus stopped on the way here,"
Papi says in his smooth clarinet voice.

"I was on the road,
working the grapes in Fresno."
He stops to take a long, slow drink.
"*Mira al chico,*" he says. "Look at Chico!"
He calls me Chico instead of Juanito, maybe
because he forgets my real name.

Papi reaches into his coat pocket and
gives me a yellow jackknife
with a drawing of a smiling man with a raccoon hat.
It's signed "Daniel Boone" in fancy letters. Papi reaches into
his other pocket. "This is from New Mexico," he says.
He hands me
a little brown cloth sack of *piñon* nuts.
Then he opens a small wooden box.

"This is the best thing on the earth!"
One of the wooden panels slides
and inside there is a golden brown glass jar
filled with syrupy honeycombs.
"*Corazón,* give me a spoon," he says.

"Felipe?"
Mami says as if pleading with him.
"You are not supposed to eat sweets."
But Papi dips the spoon into the jar anyway
and lets it slide onto his tongue.
"I like it to slip
from my lips down to my throat,"
he says, then gives me the little box.

I look down.
Don't know what to say.
It seems like I haven't seen him ever.
He's a stranger and a papi at the same time.
"Thanks, Papi," I say. Then, a knot
bubbles up to my throat.
Are we going back to Ranchito Garcia?
Is little Estevan back, is Maria Luisa there,
and Toña,
is she still throwing rocks at the roosters?
Have I been dreaming?
Where have you been?

But nothing comes out.
Papi gets up, takes a towel, "We're leaving
in the morning!" he says.
"This place is like a cemetery!
Cold and wet, gives you rheumatism,
like when I worked in the *ranchos*
of Cheyenne, Wyoming, and Denver, Colorado."
He pushes the door and
heads to the hallway shower.

EL PERRO MORNING SPECIAL

At 5:30 in the morning
we step into *El Perro;* we get our tickets.

"Do you have my oranges?" Mami says
from behind my seat. Papi sits next to her
with his white straw hat and his blue coat.
He is so quiet it's like he's not here.
The conductor in gray sits in his puffy seat
and takes up his microphone:

"This is Coach Number thirty-three eighty-two
departing for San Diego.
We'll be stopping in Fresno, Los Angeles,
and Oceanside.
Last stop San Diego,
last stop San Diego. Please
check your tickets. We'll be taking a fifteen-
minute breakfast break in Fresno and a lunch
in Los Angeles. Remember
your coach number, number thirty-three eighty-two,
thank you."

Coach thirty-three eighty-two
makes a right turn on 7th, then a left on
Mission Street. We ride up on the freeway

and cross the Bay Bridge; the yellow lights
of the tunnel seem to say, *Over here,*
Juanito; come, come.

We shoot out of the dark depot into
the blurry light and the mist swirling
through lanes of traffic, a wavy line
over the waters that grab the land.
We are heading south, as if all along
we were in a dream. Papi, Mami, and me,
once again.

I am sitting at the very front of the bus.
Mami and Papi behind.
Quieres una naranja?
"Want an orange?" Mami squeezes an orange
in between my seat and the side window.
Mami always carries a bag of oranges and lemons
when we travel; it's good for the dizzy spells.
Why does she always get dizzy spells?

Somewhere in the same bag she keeps
the photographs of Mama Grande Juanita
and Papa Grande Alejo. Wrapped tight
so they won't break.

Highway ahead, the bay to my right,
small hills to my left. I think of
Chacho with his sneaky smile, Cousin
Alvinita with her long brown hair, Cousin Tito
and his cool talk Daddy-o, the rotten bodies
lying in the Autopsy Room —
are they still there?

Back at school, I can hear
Mr. Heyden and Moses Simpson chat
about MPH, miles per hour. Honolulu shoots

a basketball over the roof at Patrick Henry;
she's taller than the basketball stand,
but she has the prettiest smile.
And Georgey Wong crab-nets on Muni Pier
making his funny faces at the seagulls.

Aunt Faustina in her dark room,
dolls with open eyes.
Uncle Lalo, his crooked laundry hands,
and Sweet Pea Price, how he dances like a butterfly
and stings like a bee. Hear
the Shark-a-coaster at Playland,
going-going-going
faster than a wolf
howling over the ocean.

"Want an orange?" Mami asks.
"No, *gracias*," I say
in a dreamy voice.

I wish we were back
at Ranchito Garcia
before the green van came.
Before I had a fight
with little Estevan on Lincoln Street.
Before we had to move.

"We are moving. That's all
I know. To San Diego," Papi says,
like he always says, because
"they have the best climate and the best
water in the whole world!"

What school will I go to?
I'll be in high fifth. Gaze out
into the highway slipping under us.
Moving-moving, fast ocean colors,
fast sky colors,
dark road colors, see
how fast they go.
I am on the Shark-a-coaster,
a rumbling ocean made of metal —
sometimes,
I can feel it climb up my chest;
then down-down-down it goes.

Rollin' in a truck, lost in a wild train
Or the Greyhound bus, trembling there.
"Where is Papi, gone again, so far away?"
Juanito asked. "When will our roads dare
Come together, so we can finally meet?"
Juanito was movin', always movin' until
One day, Juanito raced down D Street.

barrio Logan

October 1958

"It's a castle!"
Mami says as we step
up a long accordion of stairs
hauling our bags
to our new apartment.

Up, up, and up.
Papi unlocks the door.
Wooden floors, old bed, sofa by the curtains,
and El Living Room! A living room?
A floor where I can play!

Open the curtains facing west, while Mami
hangs clothes in the closet.
She pulls out rags and S.O.S. detergent
and sets it aside. "Where's my Virgen Maria?"
She remembers and opens her pink jute bag,
pulls out a little bundle.

A Virgen Maria postcard,
a bronze crucifix,
Mama Grande Juanita and
Papa Grande Alejo's photograph
just like the one in Chacho's house,
and a scarf rolled into a cigar.

"What's inside?"
I ask.

Mami unfolds the scarf.
Two night-black braids with a red ribbon
at the tail. "Your *mama grande* had the darkest hair,"
Mami says. Papi takes a drink of water
and tastes it for a few seconds. "Good-good," he says.
"San Diego has the best water!"

Mami places the braids by *la virgen.*
She lights a candle. "Don't start a fire,
okey, *corazón*," Papi says, and takes out
his Baptist Bible and places it by the bed.
He reads a few pages to himself. Closes
the thick book. Recites in a whispery voice.

"*Come tu pan con gozo,
y viviras!*
Eat your loaf of bread with joy,
and you shall live!"

Papi likes to say things like that.
I don't know if it's poetry or Bible sayings.
"We need some *comestibles!*
"Food comes first," he says, tucking the Bible away.

"First, I need to wash the kitchen
and mop the floors," Mami answers.

I stare out the window, from the second floor.
The ocean!

"I can see the ocean!" I sing.
Papi drinks another glass of water.
"I told both of you. San Diego has the best
climate in the world. And here in Logan Heights,
where the *Mejicanos* are,
just a few miles south of downtown,
you can almost taste the ocean water!"
Papi washes his hands. Mami hangs her black coat
in the bedroom closet.
She dances a little,
into El Living Room. She twirls
and hums a sweet little melody.

Luna, luna
Comiendo su tuna
Tirando las cáscaras
A la laguna

Moon, moon
Eating your prickly pear
Tossing the peelings
Into the lake over there.

Mami's eyes are full of tears,
dancing, her hands up in the air
as if playing a tambourine made of stars.
"I am so happy, Juanito," she says,
"we are all together again."

Mami dances to me, her arm
on my shoulder.
"Kearny Street," Mami says.
"Our own little street."

"Hey, you! Chico!
Wanna eat some sour grass?
Come; I'll show you."
A chubby boy with a face like Beaver Cleaver
on the *Leave It to Beaver* show — naughty
and funny at the same time —
calls to me
from the street. I am halfway up
the chopped tree in front of our apartment.

"Hey, you! Chicooo!"

"My name's not Chico!"
"Yes it is! I heard your grandpa call you that."
"He's not my grandpa!"

"Come down; come on!" he says.
"What you doing up there?"

"Ever seen the way the ocean waves
turn into flashy birds?" I ask him.

"My name's Salvador," he says.
"My friends call me Chava.
Here, have some."

Chava hands me a bouquet
of thin green grassy straws
with yellow flowery caps.
"Take a bite!"
"Tastes like lemon candy!" I say
and chomp-chomp
on a bright green rope of sour grass reeds.
"Come on!" Chava says.

We run to a burned-down house
on the corner of Kearny and Sampson Street.
"This is where Mrs. Trementina
used to live. Grandma Lola says
that she was a witch. She always
had wild cats in the house, empty bird cages,
and she lived alone with a furry crow
that ate jalapeño chile seeds
and tamales made out of rat meat!
Last Tuesday, a green puff of smoke
blew out of the roof.
Poof-poof!"

"Where is she now?"
"Dunno," Chava says, and kicks
a coil of bedsprings.

We walk by the blackened
fence and busted flowerpots to the backyard
where there is an island of fresh grass.
"See," Chava says.
"All the sour grass candy
is ours now!" I like Chava
because he likes to play in the dirt
like I used to in Ranchito Garcia.

We scoop a ton of sour grass into
our baggy pant pockets,
munch on it as if we were goats.
"Chico! Come here; hurry!"

Chava digs a hole
by a half-charred cactus.
"What is that?
Looks like a baby crocodile,"
I say. "Nah, nah." Chava
investigates with a stick.
"It's a lizard! A crispy dead lizard!
It's probably Mrs. Trementina!"
I say, "Lesgo!"

"We have to bury it!" Chava cries.
"Or else she'll come and get us at night."

Chava digs while I pinch my nose
with one hand and hold the lizard
by her charcoaled tail with the other.
Down into the hole she goes!

We pat dirt and twigs on top;
then we plant a circle of lemon
grass flowers around
the lizard grave.
"Lesgo! Lesgo!" I say.

"We have to pray first!" Chava says.
"But I don't know any prayers!"

"Come tu pan con gozo," I say
kinda low. "Nah, that's no prayer.
Let's sing 'Silent Night,' ok, Chava?"

We kneel and press our hands
over our hearts like we are saluting
the flag. . . .

Silent . . . night . . .
Holy . . . night . . .
"Hey, you two chicken heads!"
A short gray-headed man
with a scar on his cheek
pokes a broom through the fence.

"Run!" Chacho yells,
"That's Mr. Angosto!
He lives in the backyard
by your house, in a shack.
He's always sweeping
the alley, plucking fresh *guayabas*
and pomegranates
from the neighbors' branches
and snooping around. If he asks you
for something, you better run like
Dennis the Menace!
My mama says
he's a dirty, smelly old man."

Chava stuffs
sour grass into his shirt pockets.
We leap over the charred fence,
make a sharp right at Sampson
to Logan Avenue, the main street.

THE WELL-FAIR OFFICE

Well-Fair
is the place we always go when
we are new in town, which is all the time,
so we can get the well-fair check
at the beginning
of the month. It's about seventy dollars.
Papi and Mami don't have regular jobs,
so we get well-fair checks.

Mami's busy scrambling for
a piece of paper in her red plastic purse.

"Here it is. Okeh.
Well-Fair Office,
One-twenty-seven, Front Street. Okeh."
Mami reads slow in English.

"There's no jobs
for farm workers in the big towns,"
Papi always says. "If you want to be a *jardinero*
and do garden work, you need to speak good English
and you need a truck and lawn mowers.
But in big towns, there are
beautiful schools for you!"

"Lesgo," Mami says in English.
"Vámonos al Well-Fair. Andale!"

"Papi, Papi! We're going!"
I wave from the top of the backyard stairs.

Papi stands with his back to me,
sharpening his shaving knife
on a wet stone
next to Mr. Angosto's shack.
Fixing the cage-gate for the baby chicks.
Papi bought them at Gomez Feed Store
on Logan Street next to El Carrito
and the bank.

El Carrito is a one-train car restaurant.
Looks like a piece of a roller coaster
dropped out of the sky
and landed in the middle of the street.

Just yesterday, Papi paid five dollars
for a tray of twenty chicks.
"That's all the money we have,"
he told me. "But, just wait, when
these little fuzzy *muchachos* get big.
We'll eat chicken enchiladas for months!"

I don't want to go with Mami.
It's always the same thing.
We wait in line. We sit in the back of a classroom
of chairs. A man in a sardine-colored suit
shuffles out with a stack of papers
and calls, "Mrs. Lucy Valencia?"
Then we go into a tiny office
and answer questions in English,
well, Mami kinda answers them in English,
but it sounds like Spanish, so I tell
the man in the sardine suit what she means.

"Where were you born?"
"Do you have a green card?"
"Have you filled out your Alien Registration Card?"

Then, they ask you,
"Who is living with you?"
Then the man in a sardine-colored suit
stands up and says, "We will be visiting you soon;
are you sure no one else lives with you?"

Then they ask about me,
"Where was he born?"
"Why isn't his name Valencia?"
And Mami says
that she's married Common Law.

I think it means that she doesn't
have to wear a ring to prove
she's married to Papi, but Papi
gave her a ring before we moved to
San Pancho. I think he did.
Unless she put it to work.

"Okey, Juanito," Mami says,
buttoning her coat. "Lesgo!"

She adjusts her Dick Tracy glasses.
The scarf around her head is her favorite color —
7UP bottle green. She says it's the color
of hope. What's hope? Sounds like
Hop and Pop backward, like a firecracker
blowing up in your mouth that
nobody can hear.

HiGH FiFTH aT
burbank ELEMENTaRY

Mrs. Sniffins cleans her nose
with a handkerchief and calls,
"Rómulo Lopez!"
"Mary Crow!"
"Jack Silva!"

"No gum chewing in my class!
If I catch anyone chewing gum again
I will ask you to paste it on your nose,
kneel right here by the United States
map, face the wall, and stretch out your arms
with a dictionary in each hand! Y'all hear me
nice and clear?"

"Yes, Mrs. Sniffins," Mary Crow
says by herself.

I am standing at the door.
Papi wears a hat and drops me off,
says, "Here your lonche." Hands me
a wrinkled bag with a tomato sandwich
on Roman Meal wheat bread.
That's the only bread we eat because
Mami says it's good for her dizzy spells

and Papi's diabetes. He takes long strides
down the hall, opens the door
blazing with light.

I hand Mrs. Sniffins some papers
they gave Papi at the front office.
"Let's see," she says. "Wanitto Palo-mars . . .
You sit next to Jack Silva and
Karen Hayashi."

"This high fifth?" I say.
"What? Here we have only fifth, then
sixth, then you go to Memorial Junior High.
Please sit down, Wanitto. You are late
to school! School starts at eight fifteen.
Ya'hear?"

"How was school, *hijo?*"
Mami asks me.
"Did you learn a lot?
I am so proud of you!
You know, I only went to third grade."
Mami tells me her story again.

About how Mama Grande pulled her out
of class in third grade in El Paso, Texas,
because she caught her stealing candy
in a store on Stanton Street,
with one of her friends, Chole. Mami says
that Mama Grande wanted her to stay home
to take care of her and help her sell tortillas
on the streets.

"And I never went back," Mami says,
washing the dinner dishes. On the wall
by the calendar, Mami glues little articles
on How to Praise Your Child. She's always
reading little things, always showing me
the newspaper. She's a better teacher
than Mrs. Sniffins.

"Mami, can I have peanut butter sandwiches?"
"Penabodda? Of course, when *el cartón* comes in,"
she says. She calls the well-fair check
el cartón, piece of cardboard,
so people won't know what
we are talking about. But there's no
one in the room, just us.

Papi's outside talking with
Mr. Angosto, building a tiny chicken farm.
No matter where we go,
Papi has a little school of chickens
and a little piece of land, even if it isn't really his.
I wonder where my little acre is,
the one he promised.

"One day you're going to grow
into big hens, bigger than Mr. Weed's turkeys,"
he tells the little chicks.
He doesn't tell them that he has a hatchet
that flips out of his back pocket
when they start gobble-gobbling like big turkeys.
In Ranchito Garcia
Papi chopped their heads off
on a tree stump. Mami would
run after the bloody headless flappers
and trap them in a gunnysack.

Then, popsplash! She would throw them
into a pot of boiling water.

After she pulled them out, I would
pluck out the feathers and sink my hand
into their chests and pull their livers out.
Smells like rotten eggs and tomatoes.

As soon as Papi comes in,
washes his hands, and has a drink
of water in a tall cherry-colored steel glass,
Mami says,
"*Vámos* window-shopping!"

window-shopping

Night-dust softens
the chopped tree outside on the street
and turns it into a blue cactus
without needles. But,
with a candle yellow feather
hanging from one of its arms — a slice of the moon.

Sampson and Logan Street.
Make a right turn. The long
bluish sidewalk
coils up to the woolly clouds
in the steel gray light.
Papi with his hat.
Mami in a checkered green coat
and her Dick Tracy sunglasses.

Run, run!
Spin around with my hands out like stars.

Peek into store windows.
A clock on the wall by a photograph
of President Eisenhower reads 7:13.
Kids play on the street
batting a ball made of tape.

There's no mangoes
in wooden boxes on the sidewalk,
like at Yee's market on Mission Street,
or soda fountains with tree bark-colored
stools and pool-green counters
like at the St. Francis Fountain
on York Street, or
Tía Albina's Mexicatessen with trays
of ham and cheese *tortas* and little red cartons
of Christopher's Milk. There's
no Boys Club. No Coach Egan with a tattoo
on his Popeye arms.

I spin again, squint my eyes
to see if I can make Logan Street turn into
Mission Street. Spin-spin.

"Wait, Mami!"
I call out as Mami and Papi walk down
another block past Sawaya's Market
and Maya's Tortillería.
Run, run, run.

Stop!
Press my face against the glass in Sal's Goods.
There's a Schwinn bike with white tires,
an electric yellow school bus,

a dry Christmas tree with little glass needles
filled with colors and bubbles,
a Hamms Beer poster that says
"In the Land of Sky Blue Waters."

"Wait for me!" I yell, at the corner.
An electric sign with curly lights in purple
glows off and on — *La Bamba.*
It crackles. No windows,
Just a swinging wooden door.
A groggy man stumbles out,
splatters spit on the sidewalk.

Run!
Catch up to Mami and Papi.
They are standing in front of Las Cuatro Milpas,
a tiny restaurant with soft amber lights inside.
There's half a dozen people sitting. Some are bowed down
having soup from round clay bowls; about a dozen
are standing shoulder to shoulder, eating crispy tacos,
drinking pink sodas, talking and laughing
as if they lived together right next to the jukebox like
the one in El Perro. The cook flies a tortilla
onto a black pan as wide as a tire on the black steel stove.
Smells like fresh corn and fried peppery chiles
and a little like cinnamon and sweet almonds.

I wonder if they have records like "Hound Dog" and
"Stuck on You" by Elvis.

"When we get *el cartón* from El Well-Fair,
we'll come, *hijo*," Mami says.
"And we'll have anything you want, okeh?"
Papi walks ahead. He picks up
a strap of rough leather.

Papi says proudly,
"When my heels wear out, I'll hammer
pieces of this leather into the sole of the shoe.
You gotta use your *cabeza*, Chico.
But never forget your *corazón* — your heart."

We cross Crosby Street and
head to a theater, El Coronet.
Looks like a little white breadbox on the corner,
made out of Popsicle sticks.
Not like the Orpheum on Market Street.
"Luis Aguilar!" Mama says, reading a movie
poster in Spanish. "Maria Felix and Pedro
Infante! When *el cartón* comes, Juanito,
we'll go, okeh?" "Ok," I say,
and stare into the lobby where
a popcorn machine shoots gold nuggets
into a glass box.

The moon rises as we go down
a hill from El Coronet. The tiny
stores fade and we are under the
glassy blue sky by the railroad tracks.

"The air smells like fresh slices coated
with butter!" I tell Mami.

"There must be a bread factory nearby,"
Papi says.

My arms go up scooping the sky
into my mouth. Mmmmmm.

"*Mira!* Look!"
Papi says, pointing to the clouds.
"See that one? It's a bread roll! And that one!
That's a long *pan frances!* A French roll!"
I take a make-believe bite of the cloud bread.
Then I act like I am slicing the cloud bread in two.
"Want some?" I ask Mami.
She takes a little bite. "Mmmm," she says.
My stomach rumbles.
We've been eating beans, rice, and soda crackers,
for weeks. When is *el cartón* coming?

"There's San Diego,"
Papi says, looking far away,
standing by
the Kensington #11 bus stop a few feet ahead.
His long coat flaps in a windy whirl.
"El Downtown!" he says.
"That's where everything is!
They even have a *Plazita*
like in Ciudad Juárez, Chihuahua.
When I was about fifteen, I'd go there.
And I would dream one day
I'd come to *El Norte*. I'd stare
at all the people going around
and around, some with sombreros,
some with dresses, whirling
like planets. I wanted to be
a comet and cross the skies
to another world."

"Plazita?"
"Yes, Juanito," Mami says.
"That's the heart of the town, *corazón*.
They have a fountain, too!"
Papi says.
"Water is," he begins,
"precious," I say.

We go back home slow and silent.
Under the tree shadows,
swaying back and forth like canoes
made of hungry moonlight.
Turn back to El Downtown, to
a sea of starry buildings shooting up
into the blue-dark ceiling.

November 1958

poor dead

"Take that gum out of your mouth!"
Mrs. Sniffins yells at Chava.
"And you, Wanitto, stop talking all the time.
When you get your report card
there will be a note for your parents
and I will tell them . . ."

Mrs. Sniffins says a lot of words
in a row. They sound like a little train
choo-chooing.

Pop! Plop!
Chava's bubble gum snags
on his nose like a crab net.

"Ok, that's it, Salvador Sifontes!
You are going to the cloak room!
Maybe there you'll learn more than
in the classroom." Mrs. Sniffins
walks stiff like on stilts,
pulls Chava by the arm,
drags him to the cloakroom
where we keep our jackets and lunch boxes.
My lunch bag is in there at the very back

so no one will see
my Roman Meal tomato sandwich.

Mrs. Sniffins unrolls an Abraham Lincoln
photograph and tells us that
she is going to pass out paper
so we can draw a poordead of President Lincoln
and that we will show them
at the Square Dance Festival in May.
"What's a poordead?" I ask Karen Hayashi.

"Your poordead will be due tomorrow!"
Mrs. Sniffins says, and hands out the papers.

"You can use pencils, crayons,
for your poordead." "Mrs. Sniffins,"
I ask with my hand up,
"what's a poordead?"

Jack Silva, who sits behind me,
laughs. Pops my head with his knuckles.
"Portrait, stupid! Not poordead!"

"Jack!
Do you want to sit on the corner
wearing the Dunce Cap all day?
Leave Wanitto alone! And hush!"

Bend my head down,
take my pencil, and press
as hard as I can into the paper.

Black hair,
black black eyes,
black black beard,
black coat,
all in black black,
so black my poordead turns to silver
like sharp pieces of black diamonds
shooting from Lincoln's eyes.

Bliing, bliiing!
the hard bell rings.

Jack stomps out the door.
Karen and Hosea put their pencils and crayons
under their wooden desktops.

Carolyn Centers waits
to be dismissed.

Clock reads 1:30.
I am last.

"Come on, *hijo*," Mami tells me.
"Lesgo and see if we can fish some *huesos*."
"Fish some bones?"

"You know what I mean," she says.
"Lesgo to the butcher shop, by El Carrito."
"But I am working on a poordead of Abraham Lincoln."
"That's nice, *hijo*. But it'll just take a minute."

We make a right on Sampson and Logan,
pass the Bank of America, pass El Carrito,
and stop at Alvarez's Carniceria, the butcher shop.

"Tiene huesos? Para caldo.
Do you have bones? For soup,"
Mami asks.
"The best, *señora*," Mr. Alvarez says
in his blood-spattered apron.

"Cuanto? How much?"
Mami pretends she is opening
her red purse for money,
but it's empty.

"No problem, *señora*,"
Mr. Alvarez says, and pulls
his handlebar mustache.
"Money's for the meat;
bones are free!"

"I love *caldo de hueso*,"
I tell Mami as we walk out.

I love to suck out the soft reddish jelly
from the bone sockets — the *tutano*,
Mami reminds me to say it right . . . *tué-tano*, she says.
Mami hands me the white bag of large round
neck-bone pieces. We glide
down windy Logan Street.

EL Carrito

El Carrito restaurant is open.
It's like a train car filled with people
going nowhere, but they don't care.
They smile and roll fluffy tortillas
in their hands.

Looks like a little train
that dropped out of the sky
without a conductor or an engineer.
Who will drive it home?

Each little table faces one of the windows.
Each counter with twin mariachi salt- and pepper shakers.
There's a milk-shake machine and toaster
by the register box. A photograph of a curly-headed boy
playing guitar and smiling above
the Virgin Mary and a vase of flowers.

"Who's that boy?"
I say, peeking into the window.
"El Ritchie Valens," Mami says;
"he was in the *Tribune* a few months ago."
"That's Ritchie?" I ask. "The one who sings 'La Bamba'?
Jack Silva sings that song at lunchtime.

Each time he says 'Bamba,' he hits me
and Hosea on the head!"

"I am going to have to talk to your teacher!"
Mami says, and pats me on the head as we walk.
She's happy that we have *huesos* for soup.

We pass a 7UP bottle
laying in the street,
El Carrito, Mami's favorite,
dreamy rain colors,
like a river,
like a garden.

I think of the green van in Ranchito Garcia
and how my friends Maria Luisa, little Estevan, and Toña
stepped inside of it never came back.

My face looks back at me
from the shiny windows.
It stretches into a weasel face.

CHICKEN BASEBALL

This morning Papi walked to La Plazita with Mami.
El cartón finally came yesterday.

On Saturdays, I watch cartoons;
Mighty Mouse is my favorite.

Eat a bowl of steamy *avena*, mush with chunks of butter
and a cinnamon stick, chew-chew it.

"Hey, little boy,
your chickens are loooose!"
Mr. Angosto croons from way downstairs,
scratching his belly, then the side of his face.

"Come on down; I'll show you
how to play Chicken Baseball! Hurry, little boy!
Is your sourgrassy friend with you?
Chava?"

"No, his *mami* won't let him play
outside because he's always getting
into trouble. And Mami and Papi
are at the Plazita."

"That far?
We'll, I'll help you. Come on;
let's get 'em!"

Jump down two stairs at a time
in my old Roy Rogers pyjamas.

"See this branch?"
Mr. Angosto says in a rough voice.
"You take it!
Sweep it across the ground!
Instead of grand-slammin' a baseball, you
make the chickens hop-hop over the stick!
That's Chicken Baseball!"

Mr. Angosto puts his arm over my shoulder
and helps me hold the bat. Shows me how to swing.
"Down low scraping the ground, that's it!
Make the little chicks fly into the sky!

"See them," he says,
"Very, very *bonito!*" Mr. Angosto says.
Pats me on the head. "Now you do it!"

"I don't want to hurt the chickies."
"They're not chicks!" Mr. Angosto changes his voice.

High and fast, like he's on TV.
"They're Shorty-roosters!" he sings.

Swoosh! Swoosh!
Swoosh! The chicks fly, twirl in the air.
Swoosh! Pop!

One of the chickies
lies on the ground with its head twisted
and its leg broken.

"Kri-kri-kriiiiii," it sings
sadly by itself.

"Uh-oh," Mr. Angosto says.
"Let's take it into my house.
Let's take care of him."

The little chick
stretches his fuzzy head,
pecks at my thumb.

"Lay him on my bed," Mr. Angosto
says, taking off his shirt.
"Now you take off your shirt, too,"
he says. "We have to be clean,
like doctors."

"Ok," I say.
"Like doctors."

"Sit on my lap, come,"
he says. "We'll take care
of the chickie and then,
I'll show you a little Teddy Bear circus prize
that I am going to give you.
I won it in a shooting gallery."

"What are you doing?"
Papi says at the cloth door.
"What's going on here?
Get back in the house, Juan!

"And you, Angosto,
Leave my boy alone!"
Papi takes a little Teddy Bear
from his hands and throws it on the ground.
"Get the heck outta here
and never come back!"

"What are you doing down there?"
Mami asks me in the kitchen.

"The little chick had a broken leg
And, and —"

Hot water comes
from my eyes.
"I am sorry, Mami.
It's my fault.
Just like when the green van came
to Ranchito Garcia.
It's my fault —"

"It's ok, okeh . . .
shhhh," Mami says,
and hugs me. "Shhhh.
You are a smart boy.

Look what I brought you
from El Downtown."
She gives me an orange
plastic water gun.
"I bought it at Goolgorth's store,
by La Plazita."

"What happened?" Papi asks,
holding the chickies in a tray.

"Mr. Angosto said
he was going to teach me
how to play and —"

"Well, don't ever go down there again.
He's gone for now,"
Papi says, placing my shirt on my shoulder.
He takes a long drink of water, then another,
gazes out the window to the ocean —
and breathes out.

"That's it!
We're moving at the end of the month!"

"But we just moved, Felipe,
a few months ago,"
Mami says.

"And, the Square Dance Festival
is next month," I squeak.

"Angosto's going to lay around all day
on his gunnysack under the fruit trees in the alley.
He'll come back," Papi says, and takes
another drink.

Mami squints out the window
into the flat sky.
"And I just fixed the papers
at the Well-Fair Office."

AT NIGHT,
ALL CATS ARE GRAY

December 1958

AT NIGHT, ALL CATS ARE GRAY

"*En la noche,*
todos los gatos son pardos,
At night,
all the cats are gray."

Mami whispers and shivers a little
as we tiptoe out down the long stairs
to Kearny Street. "If you have spots, if you
are orange or even if you are white, at night
every kitty looks the same. No one
knows if it's you or someone else,"
Mami tells me. I jump to the last step.

Papi carries a heavy suitcase and a box on his shoulders.
Mami with her favorite pink gunnysack bag,
with photos, fruit, and Grandma Juanita's braids.
And me, with an extra-large Safeway bag of clothes
and toys. It's still dark, even though

the sun peeks
over Frosty's Ice Cream Shop and splashes
rays of light on Logan like scattered tangerine peels. We wait
for the Kensington #11 bus.

"Wait until you see the apartment, Lucha,"
Papi says. "It's on National and Crosby.
Just a block from Las Cuatro Milpas,
right next to Amador's Market, a Spanish
restaurant, and El Porvenir,
the best *tortillería* in Logan Heights."

"Ohh!"
Mami says, breathes out,
and winks at me
as if we are moving
to El Downtown.

Papi knows all the places;
he's a super walker.
If Papi had a driving license,
he could be a taxi driver.
Mami, too. She could drive the Kensington #11
to the Frosty shop before dropping me off
at Burbank Elementary.

Mami's bag pops open
and spills towels and a couple of apples.
I pick them up and catch up to Papi ahead carrying
a suitcase strapped with a belt in one hand and
the cardboard box on his shoulder
rattling with Mami's toaster and iron, cans of Pork & Beans,
my blue metal cars, and Papi's favorite Army canteen. I peek
into my Safeway bag to make sure
my net bag of cat's-eye marbles is in there
with my school notebooks and the toolbox Papi gave me.

We pass by Las Cuatro Milpas
and La Victoria store; well, it's really a house
with a Nesbitt Orange Soda sign on the screen door.
Make a left at Doria's Drugstore. "There, see?"
Papi says, resting

his cardboard box and suitcase on the curb,
takes off his hat.
"See?"

I let go of my bag like Papi.
Papers fly out on the street.
"My poordead!" I say.
"It's due today. Hurry, Mami!"

We make a right at El Porvenir,
on the corner of National Street.
Painted in turquoise — El Porvenir
Tortillería. We pass the Spanish restaurant.
"Here we are," Papi says.
Apartment Number Nine. We go up.

Papi unlocks the door with a long key
that looks like a spoon with a hole in it.
Mami runs to the kitchen and brushes
a hundred *cucarachas* from an old sheet
of butcher paper on the kitchen counter.
The cockroaches scatter on the floor.
Mami stomps-stomps.
"*Cu-ca-ra-chas,*" she says.
"*Cu-ca-ra-chas!*" Stomp-stomp!

Papi opens the windows
that face National Street.
"Nothing better than fresh ocean air," he says.
"Smells like fish," Mami says, sweeping
the cockroaches into the center of the floor.
"It's the canneries," she says,
"at the edge of the bay. You work hard,
for little pay. *Pero algo es algo.*
But at least it's something.

"I'd work there
if I didn't get these dizzy spells."
Mami gets the shredded broom again,
sweeps the dead *cucarachas* into a rolled newspaper.

"Mami, I have to go to school; my poordead is due."
"Okeh," she says, "here, twenty-five cents,
ten cents for each way and five for a bag of chips
or *saladitos,* salted plums,
at La Victoria on your way home."

I run to the bus stop
on Logan and Crosby, right across from the Coronet.
Get on, drop my money in a glass box
that turns with a wheel the size of a silver dollar
and swallows the dime. Ride

with my arm across the bench
by the open window.
My poordead in my back pocket.
The street goes under me. Clouds roll
over me. I am somewhere in between
the breeze.

"I am sorry, Wanitto,"
Mrs. Sniffins says.
"You moved! You can't go to this school anymore.
I'll take you to the principal's office, ok?"
"But my poordead?"

"Didn't your parents know?
When you move that far, you need a new school. It's ok,
Wanitto; Mr. Dillahunt will take you
to Lowell Elementary. It's one block
from where you live!"
"But the Square Dance Festival?"

Mrs. Sniffins looks
at my poordead of Abraham Lincoln.
"You know, your drawing is one
of the best I've seen. I am going to pin it
on the board for the whole class to see.
You are quite an artist! Congratulations.
Get back in that room, Silva!" she yells
from the hall.

Step out with Mr. Dillahunt.
The wind curves around my neck.
I look back at Chava staring out the window,

a ball of gum in his cheek. Karen Hayashi
waves good-bye; Jack Silva sticks out his tongue,
punches Hosea Ridley in the ear.

Going with Mr. Dillahunt down-down
Logan Street, past El Carrito
in seconds, past Las Cuatro Milpas
with a line of people pouring out the door.
"They have the best jukebox in town!" Mr. Dillahunt says
in a friendly voice. "And the best tacos! Ha!
You are lucky, boy! If I was you, I'd come here
for lunch." "Lucky?" I say; then,
we are in front of a row of green long
houses with tiny windows.

"These used to be Army barracks,"
Mr. Dillahunt says,
and fixes his red tie.
Barracks? I say to myself.
"Your new school, Wuneddo!"

Tadpole

Slumped over my desk
in Mrs. Sampson's class.
Yesterday she played "Wade in the Water"
on the phonograph. Everyone's
practicing for the Christmas assembly.

Yesterday, Mrs. Sampson
called me to sing a song.

With her bright orange dress,
she stood at the front of class
and held her hands together
as if she was praying.
"Come, my dear," she said.
When she said that, I stood up
without thinking. And I floated
to the front next to her.
Her eyes were like deer eyes
and I could feel her smile in my heart.
No one in school ever called me dear.
"Did you know you have a beautiful voice?"
Mrs. Sampson asked me.
"You're made to sing gospel!" she said
with her honey-sweet words and

her warm hand on my shoulder.
But you are only using one-third
of your voice. You got to be
one hundred percent!"

I slump because
100 is too big.
I don't know if I can
even make it to 40 percent.

Today,
Mrs. Sampson asks everyone to stand.
"Put out your hands," she says.
"Show me," she says. "They better be clean."
Stops in front of me.

Facing Mrs. Sampson,
at the back of the classroom
with my hands out as if waiting for rain
to come down from the sky and through
the roof. I am waiting for the mountains
to grow back again,
to come cracking
out of the floor
with rivers and frogs
and tadpoles in little ponds. But

I am standing alone
with my hands
out, open, full of cold
classroom light.
I am the tadpole —
the last one.

Papi says
he's leaving for the *ojos de agua*
near El Mulato, Chihuahua, again. First week of May,
"good time to make a trip," he says, shaving
from the thin bathroom.

"The water will heal you," he says.
"Why don't you go to a doctor?"
Mami says.
"All they know is knives
and pills! Water, you drink it and it cools you,
warms your heart. Cleans your liver.
Water is . . .

Precious."

"Precious," I whisper in bed
by the kerosene lamp.

Pull the bedsheet
over my mouth
and chew it.

The orange neon halos
from the Spanish restaurant

glow on the little window
next to my sofa.

The *S* in *Spanish* glows red,
turns into a snake; then it
cools icy and goes orange, then
fire white.

Sleep at my desk.

Mrs. Sampson says she's going to send
me to the principal's office again
because all I do is clown around
and sneak out of school a lot.
"Haaa!" Ralphy snickers.
"Shadup, chump!" I say.

"What did you call me?"
Mrs. Sampson says.
"Nothing, Mrs. Sampson.
I was talking to Ralphy and —"

"What did you just say, Juan?
You go right now!"

Slip out of the green
barracks and kick the sandy dust
into the principal's office and sit down.
Sit and lean back a little. Then,

bow my head and look down
at my bitten brown sad shoes.

My stomach is a knot.
Wet stuff comes down my eyes and nose.
"School's stupid," I say to myself.
"Stupid, stupid!"

"Dodge this!"
Bonk!

Ralphy bops me in the head, after school
in the playground playing dodgeball.

I am catching my breath
on a little hill by the fence.
Sometimes, at lunchtime,
I come here so I can see all the kids play,
on the sandy field. And I can hear all their voices
moving up into the sky where the clouds play
like the choir in Mrs. Sampson's class.

Next to the yonke yard —
that's where they keep busted cars
and wrinkled fenders, torn tires, and stringy engines
made out of spiderwebs and boy spit.

Sometimes when I throw the ball
over the fence I make Ralphy crawl into the yonke.

We stop at Amador's Market
on National Avenue.
Buy black wax mustaches and

red cherry wax lips, run
across the street to the Neighborhood house.
"Gonna check out a basketball,
I'll be right back," Ralphy says.

Whoosh!
Whoosh!
Swish!
Swish!
Plop!
Right into Ralphy's stomach.

"That's what you get for
hitting me with the dodgeball!"

Whoosh!
Whoose!
Plop!

We play Around the World.
Follow a chalk circle
and shoot from every angle, I miss.
Ralphy misses.
"Hey, can I play?"
Miguel Estrada from Mrs. Sampson's class
joins us. He's grinding a taco with lettuce flying
out of his mouth wild like a *piñata*.

"Where did you get that?" I ask.
"*Las Cuatro Milpas!*
Want some?"
I take a bite, Ralphy takes a bite.
Here have some Bubble Up.
We sit down for a while.
Eat and laugh and laugh.

Kerosene Lamp

Mami talks to herself
in the kitchen, washing my pants
in the sink.

"Why does he always leave?
He should go to a doctor.
Maybe he can't get used to living in the city.
He said he would stay with me to raise Juanito.
I must be strong, like my mama grande *Juanita,*
who raised all eight of us in Juárez.
He really should go to a doctor."

The kerosene lamp burns and flickers.
Lights up the ceiling; a pool of amber light
Waves and dims, grows dark, darker.

Knock! Knock! KNOCKKNOCKNOCK!
"This is the sheriff !
Telegram from San Francisco
for Mrs. Palomares!"

ORANGES AND LEMONS

Mama reads a yellow telegram,
puts one hand over her mouth.

"Your uncle Jeno,
hee-hee-he
passed away yes-ter-day,"
Mami says in between tears.

"Your uncle Arturo says that we must leave right away.
The funeral is this Sunday!" Then, quiet, silence.

Mami sits in the dark room
that she keeps as clean as the windows
facing the ocean. She breathes in long
waves and lets out a little moan
as she drops her head; then
her little shoulders tremble.

I sit next to her
and place my arms around her.

In the morning
I will pack a small paper bag, with a couple
of oranges and lemons for her.

"Your uncle Jeno was locked up
in a military hospital in San Pancho for the last
twenty years. I don't know why," Mami says
in a soft voice.

"He was the one who brought us from Mexico City
to the United States back in the twenties
when I was a child, when we had nowhere to go.

Jeno was the one with the beautiful writing."
Mama wipes away her tears, kisses my cheek.

"Let's rest a little," she says.
"We'll leave early, before the sun comes up."

En la noche,
todos los gatos
son pardos.

At night,
all the cats
are gray.

rumble seat

January 1959

Cousin Judy picks us up by the Yuba Hotel
outside El Perro, on the corner of 7th and Mission Street.
Her hair is so curly
it looks like it's made out of music notes.

The air is frosty;
people wear long thick coats. And puff-puff into their hands.
We go down Mission Street, make a left on 20th Street.

I wonder what's going to happen?
I never been to a funeral.
I never met my uncle Jeno.

Mami walks in through the front door
of La Reina Mexicatessen. Tía Albina closes the cash register
and stacks Lucky Strike cigarette packs on the counter.

"Kiss your uncle's hand,"
Mami says as we enter the room
by the large copper kettles where he mixes
the ingredients for the tortillas and Mexican candies.
The tortilla dragon is quiet, old, and gray.

"Kiss your uncle's hand; that's the proper
thing to do, Juanito," Mami says as she stands
holding her purse.

"But they'll see me,"
I say, pointing to my cousins sitting on a sofa.

"*Andale!* Hurry up!"
Mami opens her eyes wide,
screws her lips.
She does that when she runs out of words.

I kneel in front of my uncle and kiss his hand.
He touches my head.
For a second, I feel like I am home, but it feels
too much like church.

"Juanito!"
Chacho whispers behind the Tortilla Dragon.
"Come on!"
Mami nods her head, goes over to my uncle,
and sits down.

Chacho runs outside,
into the garage.
"Help me open it," he says.
We both lift the crooked door.
"The rumble seat is mine!" Chacho says.
"Climb in!"

"Hey! You dog doughnuts!
Don't even breathe on my 1938 Ford coupe!"

Cousin Beto,
who I haven't seen for a long time, says.

I remember we were living
in Ranchito Garcia when Cousin Beto
came over. "I just got out on leave, Tía,"
he told Mami. "You look so *guapo*
in your Navy uniform," Mami said,
holding his photograph.
"This is for you, Juanito." He pulled out
a box with a photo of a B-52 bomber on top.
"Let's put it together, ok?"

And we bounced on the bed of our one-room *traila*
and took out the little plastic plane twigs
and made the wings, the propellers, the cockpit,
and the rest of the body. When we were done
Cousin Beto stood up on the bed and
tied the bomber to the lightbulb.

After Cousin Beto left, every night,
before going to sleep,
I'd fill up my lungs with as much
air as I could squeeze into them
and blow-blow as hard as I could
so the B-52 could fly
far over the clouds

where I could play
with Cousin Beto, except
he wasn't my cousin anymore,
when I was up in the clouds
with him playing —
he was my father.

breath or bread

Mami picks up
a handful of dirt; softly
she moves it as if it was
made out of breath
or bread.

She throws it
down into a hole
carved in the earth
on a little hill
facing the Gallongate Bridge.

Mami looks down
as the dirt flies.
When it lands
it makes a whispery sound
on Uncle Jeno's casket.
Then, Mami falls down
and cries.

She cries
as if she is a mountain by the sea
and the ocean splashes up
to her from nowhere,
wets her,
and when it wets her,
all the hard
square stones
in that mountain
turn into
a waterfall.

black borders

February 1959

black borders

At home,
on National Avenue,
Mami pulls out the old raggedy photo album
from her pink jute bag,
opens it to a page with black borders.

"This is your uncle Jeno, with the white shirt.
This is your uncle Arturo, with the blue suit.
At the military hospital," she says.

"He did so much for us.
We used to live on the streets, in Mexico City.
In Juárez, I even had to walk to Mt. Franklin
in El Paso and beg
for leftover food from the people in big houses
and bring it all the way back to my *mami*, Juanita.
That's why I want you to go to one school
and not one hundred.
That's why we are here, Juanito."

I want to ask Mami,
"Here? Where?
Where?"

HOW TO DRINK WATER
FROM THE OCEAN

"Papi's home!
Papi's home!"

Footsteps
on the stairs.

"Be quiet! Shhhh.
What if it's the well-fair man?
Maybe they're checking on us again.
Shhh, be very quiet."

"Papi!"
I hug him for a long time.

"This is for you, Chico," he says.
"A Davy Crockett T-shirt!"
I put it on my head, like a folded crown. Act goofy.
He hands Mami a scarf
with peacocks and rivers on it.
"Ay, Felipe," she says, and puts it on.

"You know why peacocks
have rainbows in their feathers?"
Mami asks me.

"Why?" I ask.
"To remind us
that we have a rainbow in our heart
and that we must carry it
so others can see it glow."

Papi throws me a miniature flour sack
of *piñon* nuts and he takes out his favorite jar
of honeycomb honey.
"The water in Chihuahua was good," Papi says.
"It was hot and it smelled like sulfur —
that's means the water is healing you.
Water makes everything possible, Juanito."

A cockroach tiptoes on Mami's kerosene lamp.
Papi catches it in one single swipe.
He jiggles it in his hand
and throws it
out the half-open window,
toward the Spanish restaurant.

"Let's go to the ocean," he says,
"tomorrow, very early.
And I'll show you
how to drink water from the ocean."

La plazita

We take the #11 Kensington bus.
We pass El Coronet,
down 16th Street, and make a left
on Broadway into El Downtown.

Pearson Ford with long turquoise cars with super
fenders like pointed tortillas, May's Coffee Shop
and Poplar Supermarket, the Rhythm Room featuring
Sunny and the Sunlighters Tonite, Frazee's Paint Store,
newspaper stands, Walker Scott, Wightman's Used Bookstore,
the Orpheum Theatre; that's the Orpheum Theatre?
It's too small to be the Orpheum.
We pass a Nuts and Things store, "Goolgorths!" Mami says,
and points to a lady spraying herself with a new bottle
of perfume. The candy cane–colored sign says:

Woolworth's.
I say, like Mami,
"Goolgorth's."

"Your *papi* loves the Plazita!"
Mami says to me.
"This is not the beach!"
I say.
"Where's the ocean?"

"Just wait a minute.
We need to transfer to another bus."

We sit next to Papi — a breeze caresses me,
with sunlight and little drops of water from the fountain.
In the middle of La Plazita pigeons fly high
above the Grant Hotel and swoop down
around all of us, in circles,

in eights,
and sixes,
and twos.

They curl low and tumble to one side and land
at the crown of the fountain where the waters flow.

The Cabrillo Theatre at the end of the Plazita
Is showing *Bridge on the River Kwai*, and
Cat on a Hot Tin Roof.

Papi gets in line at the bus bench.
We take the R bus to Belmont Park.
We pass 2nd Street to the bay,
battleships and old dirty sailboats.
The water at the edge
of the city is a prickly *zarape*

made out of wavy cactus leaves.
A pigeon flutters across the window.

"Are those *palomas,* like *Palomares,* like
our name?" I ask Mami.

"A *paloma*
is a dove.

A dove is smooth
like cinnamon,
like baked clay,
like you, Juanito," Mami tells me.

"These are pigeons,
living in the big city.
One day, maybe
they'll be more like doves.

When we have little to eat,
when we don't have a place to live,
when we are traveling alone in the night —
that's when we are pigeons."

Fish broom

We fly across a soft bridge
and arrive at the edge of a painted white
figure 8 laying on its side, yawning,
trembling, then roaring,
the Belmont Roller Coaster.

Welcome to Belmont Amusement Park
A flag flaps high above the corner.

The Hammer Ride peeks
at us from the other side of the roller coaster.
Reminds me of Uncle Arturo's giant tortilla machine
that he kept in the basement on Harrison Street.
Except The Hammer swings its steely head
up and down. And instead
of gobbling corn dough, it rocks two children
in its mouth made of cage steel. Then,
it crashes down, flips up, and sprays
screams into the salty air.

Papi rolls up his pant legs.
Mami shakes off her shoes.
I roll up my pants like Papi.

Papi finds a broken broom on the sand,
a piece of rope, and a nail.
"What are you doing, Papi?"
"Making you your first fishing pole.
Always work with what you got, Son.
Never wait until tomorrow."

Papi hands me the fishing broom.
It looks like a long toothpick
with a noodle for a nose.
The nail dangles at the end of the noodle.

"Cool Daddy-o!" I say, and put
my fish broom on my shoulder and follow Papi.

Papi walks into the water,
well, just a little, up to his ankles.
"Here," he says.
Takes three empty jars from his coat pockets.
"For you," he tells Mami.
"And for you!"

We take another step
into the flashing foamy waters.
I think of Mrs. Sampson
and the Lowell School Spring Assembly next month.

Maybe I'll get to sing.
Turn back for a second to make sure
we don't get lost.

The roller coaster shrinks
but you can still hear kids screaming.
The sand spreads out
like a smooth sparkling fan
from the ocean.
Girls play volleyball;
big muscle guys
run after the ball
and trip on a log of seaweed.
One woman is standing
with her son; she holds him by the hand.
Both look at us as if we
are the ocean.

"You let the water come in,"
Papi says. "Let it fill your jar;
let it come in.
There's a little sand in there.
Let it settle down."

Papi holds the jar up to the sun
as if he is asking for something;

then he drinks it, spits some out,
pours the rest on his head.

"Now you do it," he tells me.
I drop my fish broom into the sand.
Bend down, touch the ocean,
the jar fills.

I reach it out to the sun;
everything is in the jar. I can tell
every little gold and silver thread,
every silvery point, they float
like all the places where I've been.
Up and down,
up and down,
they settle for a little bit.

I drink.
Let it cool me.
Salty, green ocean
swaying under the sun
at the end of the world —

Mirrors
in the waters
remind me

when I am alone
looking at myself
in the mirror in the bathroom
sometimes I see a boy
blurry and worried;
sometimes I see a boy
strong and tall.

d street, el downtown

March 1959

POOF-POOF

A bicycle man whirrs
across the front porch
on D Street.
One block from Broadway.
Five blocks from El Downtown.

Why did we have to move, Mami?
Why are we always moving?
I want to ask.

But my lips are tight.
My hands are tight.
The middle of my chest is locked up.
I can barely breathe.

Is this how my uncle Jeno felt
when he was being lowered into the ground?

Mami comes out of
our new apartment — #5.
11th and D Street.
Don't care.

"Juanito,"
she says in her churchy voice.
"Juanito, the Spanish restaurant people
bought the apartment building where we
were living on National Street.
They gave Papi a letter
with a lot of English in it. You need a lawyer
for this." Mami digs into her purse
for the letter. "Your *papi* said,
Let's get the hecka out of here!
That's all he said and then — poof!"
Mami makes a funny face.
Then a sad one.

"Papi never went to school, Juanito.
All he knows is moving, hard work,
like when he was in the fields, Fresno,
picking grapes, then cotton, then tomatoes,
then melons, then broccoli, then apples in Washington,
then grapes again — in Fresno.
That's where you were born, ten miles south,
in Fowler. I was picking peaches a few days
before you were born. Now, we are on this street,
in El Downtown, we in El Downtown now,
on D Street! Things will get better,
and the library is just a few blocks from here;

you can take the bus to school, on Broadway,
one block from here, see?"

"Bu-bu-but
I was-was-going-going
to-to-get-to-go
be in the school assembly,
uh-uh,
I never get to finish anything and when I go to class
I never get to start anything because everyone
is already done!"

Mami drops her purse on the porch
next to the bare wall. Sings me a little song,
the song she used to sing to me
when we lived in Ramona Mountain.

"Adios, mi chaparrita
Que ya se va tu Pancho
Mas allá del rancho
Y muy pronto volvera. . . ."

I plug my ears.

When I unplug my ears
I hear a girl's voice singing
"La Bamba" out loud with music playing
in the next apartment.

We are in #5.
Who's in #7?

KESSLER'S MESSENGER SERVICE

Sit on the stairs outside.
Gray stairs that face a gray wall across the street.
Cars melt as they fly through D Street to Broadway
one block to the right.

The warehouse wall reads
Kessler's Messenger Service.
A man on a gray bicycle pedals out of a door
with a bag of mail on his back
and he's gone, in between cars and trucks
pumping pillows of smoke into the air.

Sitting.
Sitting.

Papi said, "We are close to El Downtown,
to La Plazita, close to the green fountain where birds bathe,
wet their wings, and fly." He said,
"You can see the tallest building in San Diego from here,
El Cortez! It's like a torch,
everyone will know you are here!"

Slow-walk down D Street half a block.
Pep Boys Auto Store —

Manny, Moe, and Jack,
that's what the sign says.
They sell car stuff, batteries and tires.
A man slides under a car in the parking lot.
His legs make an *x*. He grabs a wrench
by his legs and makes tapping sounds.

Tappity-tap-tap!
Just me and the melting cars,
the sidewalk and a puddle of yellow grass.

Don't want to go to a new school again.
Told Mami I am sick,
so she brings me more comic books,
Little Lotta and *Richie Ritch*.
I tell her to bring me the *Hit Parade*,
where they have all the words to the songs
on the radio, like "Chantilly Lace" and
"Just a Dream" by Jimmy Clanton.
I saw him on the Dick Clark *Bandstand* show.
All the kids swing each other around the air
like little Ferris wheels.

And they are always smiling.
Dick Clark asks their names
and shakes their hands.
Boys and girls

move close to each other
in front of the TV cameras
and shake their hips
and kick their feet like grasshoppers.
They don't kiss each other's hands,
and it's not like dodgeball.

Walk up to the mailbox
outside by our apartment.
A letter?
What's it doing in there?
A letter? Made out of a torn newspaper?
Without a stamp?

To: Chico #5
From: Maria #7

March 20

Hi, Chico . . .

Do you have any school paper?
Can I borrow some?
My father says I can't
walk to the store by myself.

Chico, right?
I heard your papi call you that.
Yesterday when you stayed up late
watching TV. These walls are made out
of thin-thin potato chips, huh.

Please don't show this note to anyone, ok?
I am not supposed to go out of our apartment
and speak to any boys. That's what Papi Ambrosio says.
Do you go to Roosevelt Elementary?
I haven't seen you there?
What room are you in? I am in #22.
Do you know how to take the Bus #7?

You can slide the paper under my door after
4:00. If you put it in the mailbox, I'll get
in trouble. That's when Papi Ambrosio leaves
to work at Hotel Circle. He's a waiter
at the Pickwick Hotel.
He comes home at 1:30 in the morning.

> *Thanks, Chico boy,*
> *Maria, Apartment #7*

MY NAME IS NOT CHICO

My name is not Chico.
Or Wanitto, or Whinnytoe,
or Wuneddo. Why can't anybody
say it right, like Mami?

I take five sheets of blue-lined school paper
that Mami bought for me at Goolgorth's.
Fold it. And scribble:

Hi, Maria, *March 21*

Here's the paper.
You don't have to pay me.
Are you going to be an argitect? Mrs. Sampson
at Lowell School
said that argitects draw the plans
for buildings. They use a lot of big paper.
How do you get to Bus #7?
Mami doesn't know.

Thanks, Maria girl,
Frankie

P.S. My name is Frankie, not Chico. Frankie, like Frankie
Avalon, you know, the guy who sings, "Gingerbread"?

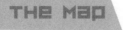

March 22

Hi Frankie Boy,

That's a nice name.
I never heard your mom call you that.
Why does she call you Juanito?
Dunno.

Here's the map to the bus stop.
If you see me, please don't talk to me.
My father takes me to school every morning.
He's always grumpy because he needs more sleep.
You'll know it's me because
I have a Roy Rogers lunch pail
and a big yellow bag of
books from the library on E Street.
Did you see American Bandstand *last week?*
Paul Anka sang "Put Your Head on My Shoulder."
That's my favorite. What's yours?

Maria #7

P.S. Thanks for the paper.
P.S. #2. I liked Chico better.

Mami and me follow Maria's map.
But there's nobody at the bus stop.
"It's time to register," Mami said.
And I don't want to go to the wrong school again.

We step onto the bus. I see a girl sitting in the back
dressed in a long wine-colored dress.
"Maria?" I say fast.

She turns away, pops her gum.
"Mami," I say,
"call me Frankie from now on.
Papi's always calling me Chico.
That's not my name."

"Your real name is John," she tells me.
"John?"
"Yes, Juanito. I named you
after your grandmother, Juanita.
But in English. It sounds so pretty,
John-john!"
"John?"

Leaves and shadows brush the bus window.
A park, a hospital, a museum, and the mountains

from far away — they float by us.
"That's Balboa Parque!" Mami says.
"It has a zoo and a fountain as big
as a circus tent. I read it
in the newspaper."

All the trees and grass
remind me of Ranchito Garcia,
planting corn with Papi,
collecting butterflies, drying pumpkin seeds
as big as your thumbnails.

Then I daydream a little, think of Chacho
telling me not to give away what I have.
But what do I have?
And Coach Egan spitting
in my face with his tobacco tongue —

Hit the floor with all you got!

HOLDING PEBBLES

After I get signed in,
run to Room #3-B.

Students are holding pebbles in their hands,
sniffing them. One boy bites one.
"Trainer, please don't put that in your mouth.
That's an igneous rock, right, children?"

"Oh, excuse me," the teacher says to me.
"I am Dr. Rossi. Welcome to class."

"Look, Papi!
This is a sedimentary rock!

"And this is a meta, meta, uh, I forgot,
but this one is an inkious rock, I mean
an igneous rock. Igneous," I repeat
like Dr. Rossi told me.
"An igneous rock is a fire-rock, like lava!
This is my rock collection for class!
I never had a tray of rocks," I tell Papi.

"Just a minute, Chico, eh?"
Papi is on the chair, bent down.
In one hand, a Gillette shaving razor, brand-new,
the little cardboard wrapper
on the floor.

Grabs his big toe, chokes it
with his other hand. Snip-Snip.
Papi chips the tip of his toenail.
He puts on a pair of glasses like the ones
Mami bought at Goolgorth's for $1.50.

Snip-snip — ay!
"Get me a towel and alcohol, Chico,"
he says in a breathy voice.
A small pool of blood spreads on the floor.
"Hurry!"

a day Later

A day later,
Papi's foot is still bleeding.

A week later,
Papi's foot is turning blue and purple.

red scooter

April 1959

It's after seven in the evening.
Knock on Door #7.

Knockkity-knock!
Nothing. Just television voices
so small they sound like crickets.
Knockitty-knock-knockitty!

Footsteps.
Another footstep.
"Who is it?"

"Chico . . . uh, I mean Frankie!"
"Frankie? You mean Chico?"
"Yes, uh, Frankie, I mean Chico!

"Uh, my mom took my *papi*
to the hospital this morning. And uh,
they haven't come back.
Where is the hospital?
Maybe they're lost."

The dark red-brown door opens.
A small hand, then long black hair,
then eyes as wide as butterflies.

"Do you like Paul Anka?"
Maria asks me.

"Look,
here's a single with his song, 'Lonely Boy.'
I'd play it, but I don't have a record player.
When the music comes on the television,
I turn it loud.
And thanks for the copy
of the *Hit Parade*. Right now I am learning
the words for 'Lonely Teardrops' by Jackie Wilson!"

"That's my favorite!" I tell her.
I leap up like a seal and spin on one foot
and do the splits, but I can't go
all the way down like Jackie.
Maria giggles.

"You better be careful or you're going to break
your legs." She laughs again.

"What's that?"
I point to a rusty photograph
on the wall with sentences
in thick black ink letters.

Alma de mi vida
Para siempre

"That's my *Mami. Alma,* it says,
You are in my heart, forever.
Can you read Spanish?" Maria asks me.

"I think I used to
back in Ranchito Garcia
in Ramona Mountain.
Mami taught me from an old
first-grade primer she found
in a store. It had songs like
'Allá en el rancho grande'
like the *Hit Parade!*"

From the middle of the bed
Maria looks back up to the photograph.
I notice the dark circles under her eyes.

"My *mami* lives in Tijuana,
in *Colonia 24,* with my sister Neli
and my brothers José Manuel,
Hector, and Jorgito."

"Why aren't they here
with you?"

"Well, Papi says,
'Shhhhh.
We don't have *papers.*'"

"Papers? Writing paper?
You want to borrow some more?"

"No, Chico, I mean Frankie,
papers! You know, when they stop
you *en la linea,* and they ask you,
'Are you an American citizen?'
And you say . . . ?

"'No, *señor.*'
Then they ask you for your
papers."

"Oh . . . papers.
Not school papers, huh?
Like a green card?" I say.
"Mami has one.
Papi doesn't."

Maria sighs. Takes a deep breath.
Her long hair falls down her
shoulders and then grows darker.

"I don't have papers," she says.
"That's why I can't go out too much.

"Want a Dad's root beer?
Or a Thunderbird?"
"Thunderbird?"
"Yeah, that's what Papi drinks
when he comes home from the hotel."
"I've never tried it.
What kind of soda is that?"
"Wine soda," Maria says.
"Root beer," I say.
"Root-root beer!" Maria laughs.

Knock! Knock-knock!
"Shhhh," Maria says.
"What if it's your Papi, Ambrosio?
Maybe he forgot his napkins?"
"What time is it?"
"It's only 10:30."

"Juan?"
"Oh no! That's my mother!"
"Juan! Come here right now!"

YELLOW TONGUE

"Your *papi* is staying in the hospital
for a few days,"
Mami says,
sitting on a 7UP bottle green *zarape*
on her soft bed.

"Why?
Are they going to cut the rest of his toenails?"
Mami puts her arm around me.

We sit on the bed
in the dark room with the kerosene lamp
licking the ceiling with its yellow tongue.

"Juanito, they are going to have to amputate his leg."
"Amfutate?" "No, Juanito, amputate.

"That means that they are going to have to cut off
his leg. A terrible infection. Gangrene.
His diabetes is so bad that his blood

reaches his feet very slowly. He can't heal well.
But he never listens. And he never visits the doctor.
How's he going to walk?"

But how's he going to go to the Plazita every morning?
How's he going to find water?

red scooter

I slump and drag my feet
down Broadway to Frazee's Paints.
There's a red scooter on a stand
inside the window. A model Navy ship, too.
Like the ones by the bay.

WIN A 1959 ZEPHYR SCOOTER!
FRAZEE'S ANNUAL SPRING PAINT SALE PRIZE.
The fast little sign spins on top of a box.

Walk in,
fill out the form:
J. Frankie Palomares
1911 D Street #5
San Diego, Ca. 92101

I let out a deep breath
and imagine Papi on the front seat of the scooter,
Mami on the backseat. Me and Maria follow
by the sidewalk, guessing song titles.

Heh-heh, I laugh a little.
Sigh a little.
Slow walk home.

BUILD A LEG

Two weeks later,

Papi spins his wheelchair
into little lines and circles, from the bed
to the kitchen, down the hall.

From the hall to the porch.
Back again.
"You got to work with what you got, Son!
Never give up!"

Papi says he's going to build himself a leg
out of plywood. But he won't.
He just says things now and stares out the window.
He doesn't go anywhere anymore.
No Plazita, no fountain.
No water.
Papi doesn't even shave anymore.

"Gonna build myself a leg, Chico.
All I need is a few supplies
from the Smarty's Hardware Store on 5th Street.
Eh, maybe you can come with me? Eh?"

When I come home from Roosevelt,
Papi's there. On the porch
squinting at Kessler's gray walls
across the street.

Maybe I can shave him.
But I don't want to cut him.
He'll get an infection
and they'll have to cut off his nose.

Papi watches a man across the street
hop onto his gray bicycle,
rear up the front wheel
like a wild horse, and race away on D Street.

Today,
coming home from school, Papi said,
"Chico, I'll race you to the Plazita!"

Papi swings his arms fast-fast and bumps
into Mami's kerosene lamp. "Oh-oh!"
Mami says, picks up the pieces
from the floor.

Good thing the lamp
was almost empty.
"We'll go to Goolgorth's and get another one, Felipe."

"It's ok, Papi," I say.
Look into his reddish eyes.
He turns to the porch and leaves.

Go inside,
make peanut butter sandwiches with soda crackers.
Run to the porch and give Papi a tray of crackers,

little tall peanut butter buildings.
Sit on the porch. Tell him about the red scooter
and how we can all ride on it. Papi sighs.
Crack crackle.
Crackers.

doña Clementina Lucero Osorio

After school,
Papi's on the porch
with his Baptist Bible.
Mami's inside
cleaning.
Get Papi a glass of water
and walk back.

Door #4 is open.
An old woman in a long silvery black dress
sits in front of a round mirror
and paints her cheeks
with a tiny gold brush.

"I used to be
a singer in Las Palmas in Logan Heights.
Back in the forties when the barrio was alive."
She speaks into the mirror.
"Clementina Lucero Osorio, La Generala!
My stage name. Me, The General! Ha!
See my guitar? Here, see?
Ever hear of Luis Aguilar?
Antonio Aguilar? Lucha Villa?
They sang with me. When they passed

through La Logan, they would stop
at La Palma. Ask my guitar,
if you don't believe me, Chico.
This guitar hears everything.
And it never forgets.
Whenever you are feeling sad
all you have to do
is pick it up — hold it
close to your heart
until
it becomes your heart, too,
because you are both moving
like dance partners!"

Doña Clemetina Lucero Osorio
slides her guitar back into the case.
There's a crooked bird cage
by her bed, with the little door open.
Is she Mrs. Trementina?
From Kearny Street? Or is she
Clementina? Dunno.
She twirls a lipstick tube
and paints her lips. Then,
she comes to me.

Closes the door.

okinawa

"To the Plazita?" Papi says, feeling
his scratchy chin.

Mami pushes him across Broadway.
Papi blinks at the wide-open street
as if he just arrived from another country.
I notice how Mami grips the wheelchair
and how she makes sure the wheels
roll over the curb. I notice how the sun
paints her dark coat with feathers of light.
Today, Papi goes out for the first time, I say
under my breath.
Will he make it across the street?

We pass the Nuts and Things House,
buy some cherry red peanuts
and a bag of popcorn.

Mami turns the wheelchair
up the curb, by La Plazita, then it rolls back.
Up again, with the red light.
Mami finds a way. She's stronger than I thought.
She spins Papi around and pulls the chair
back-back, up, up.
I help her lift it to the curb.

A sailor in blues helps, too.
A tattoo on his arm —
OKINAWA.

"Many blocks
to Okinawa?"
Papi jokes.

"It's far," the sailor says, "but close."
Then he points to his heart.

That's how I feel about Papi sometimes.
Far, but close. Today I feel closer.

The sky is blue-gray now,
clouds low and airy.
"Let's go to the fountain, Chico."
Papi races ahead of me.

The clouds open and the sun falls
on the little block, La Plazita
in the middle of El Downtown.

Pull out my gold ring
from my pocket.
Have it clipped to my pants with
Mami's safety pin. Slip it on

my finger and dip my hand into
the fountain waters to make a wish.
It flashes like a star.

I wish
that Papi gets better.
I wish
that Papi stays and that we don't have to move,
well, at least until I finish school.

Wave, wave
both hands in the water.
Then,
my ring slips,
falls,
and turns and lands on
bright copper pennies; then it rolls away,
disappears.
From the dark green fountain waters
mist comes up and wets my face.

La Visita

Mami is making a tray of of her famous
"Apartment Enchiladas."

"Apartment Enchiladas
are easy," she says, holding up a yellow can
of El Pato Enchilada Sauce.

"You pour the sauce, Juanito,
into the saucepan, make sure it is hot.
Then, add a little oil, garlic.
Let it stew. Get another pan; add oil.
Dip a tortilla in the saucepan,
make sure the sauce covers it, and then —"

KNOCK-KNOCK!
Knockitty-knock-KNOCK!

Mami peeks through a little glass eye
in the middle of the door.

There's a young man dressed in a suit
and a woman, all fancy dressed, too!
She whispers,
"Maybe it's the people from El Well-Fair.
They're coming to check on who's living here."

"Open it, Mom!
Maybe I won a prize!
Maybe I won the red scooter from Frazee's!
Open it!"

"Hello?"
a man in a navy blue suit says.
"We are here to visit our father.
My name is Antonio Palomares and this is Dominga."
"Yes, come in; I sent you a letter
saying that he was having an operation," Mami says.

"Papa?"
the woman in the leafy purple dress says.
She doesn't smile. Her hair curls down to her neck
and her eyes are sad.
She barely touches Papi's shoulder and sits down
on the bed.

"Papa?"
I say to myself.

down the hall

Inside the community
bathroom, down the hall, I close the door,
look at myself in the mirror.

"You're gonna knock out
Sweet Pea Price!
You! Are gonna knock out Sweet Pea!" I say
with the faucet puffing
hot steam into the chipped sink bowl.

Mami just told me
that when Papi goes to
the *ojos de agua*, in Mexico, he visits his old family.
She says that Papi had a different life a long time ago.
She says that she was going to tell me when I got older.
She says that we are Papi's family now.

My heart is hiding.
Wish it would beat a little.
Wish I had Doña Osorio's guitar so I could hear it.

You're gonna knock out
Sweet Pea Price!
Pow!
Pow-pow!

dr. rossi talks about diamonds

"A diamond is nothing but coal
that survives incredible pressure!"
Dr. Rossi shoots a slide
on a screen. "See?

"Gold is hidden
inside black tunnels
of earth.

"What is precious today
once was simple, ordinary stuff,"
Dr. Rossi says, passing around
a tiny crystal diamond speck in a box.

"What about us? Are we like diamonds
or like coal?" Anita Green, to my right, asks.
She curls her red hair with her fingers.
"That question is worth more than gold,"
Dr. Rossi says.

I look into the little diamond's face.
It shines in every direction, even when I cover it
with both of my hands.

roller coaster

Hi, Frankie Chico Juanito!

Got your cute drawing
of the Red Scooter with gold flames
sparkling on the sides. Thanks!
Red and gold are my favorite colors, too!

My father will be working all day Saturday.
Let's play. I'll show you some songs I wrote, too.

Bye
Maria #7

Antonio and Dominga left this morning.
Antonio didn't even say hello.
Didn't even look at Mami
when she brought him a cup
of her favorite *Te de Yerba Buena.*

Dominga said to call her Sally
and asked me if I like school.
Said she always wondered about me.
"Write me," she said.
She took me to Frazee's
and bought me the model Navy ship —
USS *Independence.*
"Take your time, Chico," she said.
"One by one, put all the pieces together
little by little. Every piece
is important," she said.

Sally laughed when I told her
my cool Daddy-o name was Frankie. She said hers was Venus.
"That's the name of one of Frankie Avalon's songs!"

"Yes, I know," Dominga said, and held my hand
as we walked back to D Street.
Maybe she *is* my sister. Well, my half sister.
Just maybe, I'll see her again —

if we stay here.

silver thread

Papi's back in the hospital.
More gangrene.
They'll probably have to anfutate his other leg.
Papi who always loved to move
and go places, see new things.

Mami says I don't have to visit Papi
if I don't want to. Hospitals make my chest
feel nervous, like when I went on a morgue run
in San Pancho and saw all the guts of the bodies.

Before I went to Roosevelt Elementary
I went to see the doctor. I had an earache.
The doctor pumped a hot glass tube
into my ear. Then the nurse
said I had to have an examination.
The doctor hit my knee with
a tiny pink rubber ax. My foot popped up.
A silver thread-thin needle
boiled in tank of water.
The doctor cleaned it and screwed it
into a glass roller.
"This is for your vaccination," he said,
and drove the needle into
the side of my left arm.

I could feel a little river of ants
crawl up my shoulder —
"Ouch! Ouch!"
each little ant said.

I am not going to the hospital.
Maybe Papi has needles all around him
and tubes in his ears and hammers
on his legs, except I forgot:
He doesn't have legs anymore.

alma de mi vida

"Maria . . .
Maria, it's Saturday!"
I whisper and knock.

"Come,
let's go to the roller coasters on the beach!
Bring your Thunderbird soda,"
I tell her. She opens the door, slow-slow
as if she was opening a mountain.

"Sit down," she says.
In the kitchenette, Maria looks up
at her mother's photograph.
"Alma de mi vida
Para siempre."
She reads it again.
"Can I go? Is it ok?" she asks.
"Can I go, Mama Alma?"

The sunshine pours through
and the breeze opens the curtains a little.
Stands on a chair, kisses
the photo, "Thank you," she says.
"Gracias."

"Ok," she says. "Ok, Frankie."
Maria climbs another chair,
grabs Thunderbird wine soda from the top
of the refrigerator. Packs it into
an old metal lunch pail, "It's my father's.
He puts his tips into it; then he sends
the money to mama. But it's empty today.

"Do you think
they'll catch me at the beach?"
she asks me.
"The men in the green van?"
she says.

"You've seen
the green van, too?" I say.

THE GREEN VAN

"One day," I tell Maria,
"at Ranchito Garcia Papi told me
to feed the pigs in the backyard.
They weren't ours.
They belonged to the Garcias.
We were taking care of the *ranchito*
for them. That's why we lived
in the *traila* in the back. I was playing
with little Eddy, and Maria Luisa.
She —" I stall a little. "She, uh
gave me a kiss on the ear because
I threw a rock at Smoky, her cat.
Toña sat in the middle of the pumpkins,
playing with her pigtails, and
little Esteban was trying to catch tadpoles
in the creek.
So, I ran up the road to see if
I could catch tadpoles, too,
with one of Papi's old leathery shoes.
The water was kinda green and
it poured out of the lace holes, but
the tadpoles stayed inside the shoe.
Little Esteban grabbed my tadpole shoe
and pushed me into the water.

It was getting late; the moon
was turning orange and getting fat.
Smoky, Maria's cat, crept along the creek bank,
meowing, pawing his head.
Little Esteban ran away from me
and threw my tadpole shoe
into the middle of the road.
Papi always told me not to make trouble.
Told me to tell him
when something was wrong. But,
but he wasn't there; he was away like always.
So, I socked little Esteban in the arm. Hard.
We were wrestling in the middle of the road
when two frosty yellow lights crawled up to us.
A door creaked open. Little Esteban shot up
and ran home.
A man with a round sombrero
stepped out and asked me,
'Do you know who lives there? There!
In that house next to that old trailer?'
'I live in the *traila*,' I said.
'Who lives in the house?'
'*Los Gar-cias*,' I stuttered.
'Emiliano Garcia? Emiliano Garcia!
We caught them again, Bryant!'
the round hat man said to the driver man.

Then, the green van drove down
our little sandy road, stopped by the house, slow.
One by one, the round hat men
pulled the Garcias from their house
and pushed them into the van.
Mr. Garcia
with his sombrero tilted to one side.
Mrs. Irma Garcia
with a bag of clothes.
Maria Luisa with
Smoky yawning in her arms.
Fat Eddy and his baggy, muddy pants.
Toña with her big eyes looking at me.
Little Esteban, crying, crying
with his head bowed down.
Two weeks later,
men with white shirts came
and boarded the windows and the door.
Papi returned three days later.
'Mr. Garcia had asked me
if we wanted to buy his place
not too long ago. With what money?' Papi said
as we walked
all the way to El Perro
in Ramona Mountain,
at a little gasoline stop at the end of Lincoln Street.

Papi said it as if
all of Ramona Mountain was falling down
and nothing could ever
lift it up again."

"It's ok, Juanito,"
Maria says in a quiet voice.
"S'ok, the Garcias will find a way
to come back. Ok?"

I stall again, my eyes
heavy —
"No, it's not ok!

"If Papi would have been here!
If I would have stayed in the *traila!*
If I hadn't gotten into a fight with little Esteban!
Everything would be ok!
Ok? Ok?
We would still be
in Ranchito Garcia!"

Maria sits quiet
Her eyes are heavy, too.
She looks at me.

Then, she looks up
at her *mami's* photograph.

Maria slips down from the chair,
turns on the radio.
"Let's dance," she says.
"Huh?"
"Let's dance, Juanito.
You just can't sit there, silly,
listen to music all your life,
and never dance! I do it all the time
in front of the mirror!"

Maria sways to a song by
The Drifters, but I am
still standing, doing nothing.

Like a bird — light, alive —
that's how Maria feels,
made of breathy feathers.
Going round, my feet stiff,
my back a little like wood.

"Come on," Maria says. "Everything
is going to be all right." She smiles
a little as we spin
saying nothing to each other
the way clouds say nothing
to the sky before it rains.

DOUGHNUT WHEELS

Maria and I
jump off the R bus.

Crackity-crack, crack.
Little steel doughnut wheels
clank up the wooden mountain
of the roller coaster in Belmont Amusement Park.
Klik-klip-klik-
klip-klipklipkip!

"I come here all the time!" I tell Maria.
"See that roller coaster?
And The Hammer, that's the meanest
ride on the planet.
You go up inside a metal cage.
There's two cages, one for each seat.
Then, The Hammer smashes you
in the air, up and down,
until-your-guts-pop-out-of-your-ears!"
I say it real fast.

Zoooooom
Ayyyyyy ayyyy ayyyyy
Uuuuh uuuh uuuuuuh Ayyyyyyy!

Voices fly out of the roller-coaster sky
like ribbons floating and falling through the wooden
boards and on the suntanned tourist noses
sniffing by.

KILÓMETRO 24

May 1959

KILÓMETRO 24

Maria #7 is leaving.

Her *papi*, Ambrosio, said,

"Maria, how many times have I told you? What do you think I can do if they get you? Don't you know they'll pick you up and then they'll come and get me? You know we don't have papers. How is your mother going to eat? What do you think you were doing at the beach? You looked like a crazy doll. All painted up. Your hair a mess. Your dress torn. It's that Frankie boy. I already told his father, that poor man! And you, little *señorita*, yes, you! You are going back to the *mercado* where your mother sells chile powder. Since you are not hungry for books, maybe a little chile powder will get your taste buds working? That's where you are headed, young lady. You are fourteen already! Should know better! You are going back to Colonia Kilómetro 24. Yes, I know it's not the best part of town and that it's just a make-yourself-a-house-with-what-you-can-find and that it's right next to the Highway 24 on the way to Ensenada, but it's home! Understand? You'll see if you have time to play there! Even the five-year-olds work until midnight selling Chiclets. That's how I started, you know? When I was seven, I used to sell little packs of gum to the tourists on the street. My father used to tell me, 'Don't come back home until you sold them all.' Ay, Maria, Maria, get in the car and stop rubbing your eyes!"

Maria is in the backseat.
She looks away, touches her cheeks
with a napkin.
Mr. Ambrosio speeds away
in their old rusty car. It wobbles down D Street,
makes a right on Broadway.

I sit down by the porch
facing D Street
in the middle of Sunday.

"D street," I say.
"D street!
Dumb Street!
Dumb!"

THE PHARAOH

Papi asks me to shave him.

Halfway down his knees
his legs are soft stumps
wrapped in white cloth.
Mami rubs medicine
on them every night.

It's been a while since
Maria left and the taxi brought Papi home
from the hospital.

I only say a few things.
"Hi, Papi. Bye, Papi.
I gotta go."

Or,
"I am going to school.
I got homework."

Today I am going to say,
"I don't have time to shave you
I am going to the library
on E Street; it's just a block

from Salazar's Restaurant."
But I don't say anything.
I want to, but my words
are locked up in a steel
box on the left side of my chest.

Mami's in the kitchen
making Papi's favorite:
fried potatoes and steak
with white gravy and
flour tortillas as big
as the carpet — well, if we
had one.

No words.
Just library books
in my hands.
I check them out, but
I don't read them.
Flip through the pages
and stare.

One book
is on Ramses the Pharaoh of Egypt.

It has pictures of his mummy.
His body dried up into gold flakes
and rubber band muscles,
mouth open wide
as if drowning in an ocean
of sad and sour sand.

EMPTY-HANDED

"Come on, Juanito.
Don't clam up," Papi says.
"Look!"

Papi slides off his wheelchair
and hops and drags himself
to the kitchen with his hands.

"Come on!" he says, while I pretend
I am reading the *Hit Parade.*
"Lesgo to Smarty's Hardware Store!
I have an idea."

Papi drags himself back and swings
to the bed, climbs up.
Leans over to a drawer.
Takes out his shaving kit.

"I know, I know," I say.
"You are going to get a hammer and wood
to make legs, I know."

"Maybe . . . maybe not!"
Papi says, playing with me.

"Maybe," he says, "I'll build a car
and we'll travel to . . . uh . . ."

"Ranchito Garcia?"
Mami says, roasting chiles
on the grill of the stove.
"Sure," Papi says.
"What do you think, Juanito?
Wanna drive?" He laughs a little.

I don't say anything.
Dead, shaky silence on my face.

Papi slides back into his wheelchair,
grabs his shaving brush.
Wets it in a steel pan of hot water
and sweeps it over a round soap tablet
in a white coffee mug until the brush hairs
are foamy. The foam covers his jaw and
he begins to scrape the knife
against his skin.

"It was your fault
we had to leave!" I yell out.

"What is it, Son?"
Papi asks.

"You told me that if I
got in trouble you'd be there," I tell him.

"Uh-huh."
Papi pulls the blade across his cheek.

"And you said that
I shouldn't get into fights!"
"Uh-huh,
uh-huh."

"But you weren't there!"
"Where, Son?"
"You weren't at the *traila*
when the green van came!
You were with Antonio and Dominga!"

"Juan, don't raise your voice
at your *papi!*" Mami says.

"That's when I got into a fight with Esteban
and punched him on the arm."
"Well, Son, I —
Ouch!"
Papi scrapes his nose
and a little blood trickles into his soapy beard.
Mami rushes over,

cleans his face,
stops the bleeding with a cotton ball.

"Yes, Son, I was with my grown children,"
Papi says, squeezing the cotton ball against his nose.
"Mr. Garcia had asked me if
I wanted to buy the *ranchito*.
Two thousand dollars, he said. All I had was the little I got
from the well-fair. So I asked my grown children,
Antonio and Dominga, if
they would lend me the money."

"What did they say, Papi?"
I ask without thinking.

"They had a bad year, they said,
the crops, their farm, didn't do well.
Maybe they felt
the same way you do. That I wasn't there for them, either.
So, I came back to Ranchito Garcia empty-handed.
I wanted Ranchito Garcia
for you, Juanito. I wanted to leave you
something. When I go back to visit
Antonio and Dominga
I miss you a lot.
It isn't easy having two families.

I didn't want to tell you.
You were too little for all these things."

Softly, I say,
"If I
hadn't
punched little Esteban,
the green van
wouldn't have
come and we
would still be
in Ranchito . . . Gar —"

The box inside my throat snaps.
Can't finish saying "Garcia."
Hot water in my eyes
rolls down my cheeks; I don't want to . . .

"I don't want to be a chump
like Chacho said!" I say out loud.
"But that's all I am!"

Papi opens his arms
in his black wheelchair
and rolls over to me.
I walk toward Mami but

Papi rolls faster.
I run across the room.
Papi swings around,
almost topples over me.
Mami comes over and
lifts Papi. "Are you two ok?"
I almost laugh, but my laugh
sounds like a cry.

"It wasn't you, *hijo;*
it was me. . . . I am
so sorry, Juanito.
I love you, Son;
you are my only one now.
And I promise
never to leave you

again."

SHAVE?

"Shave?"
Papi says.

My arms go up
by themselves and they wrap
around Papi's shoulders.
My cheeks rub against Papi's rough face.
Wiry sideburns. He feels hot
like his heart is right next to mine.
Beating and breathing into me.

We're back
from Smarty's Hardware on 5th Sreet
by the pawnshops selling silver rings and
star-splashed guitars that the sailors
put to work when they come off the ships.
Papi's got a bag of nails
and four long sticks of wood.

Mama said I would look
good playing a saxophone. "I want
to be a flute player," she said.
"That's what the angels play in the heavens."

Papi makes a funny face. "You are my angel,"
he croons. Mami said
that if I would walk into Apex Music
on Pawnshop Row, by myself,
and ask about saxophone lessons
she would give me three dollars to put the sax
on layaway. What's layaway anyway?

I think they lay the saxophone down
on a little bed until you are ready
to pick it up.

Papi said, "Lesgo."
"My son wants to learn to play, *señor.*
Señor, this is my son, Juanito; he studies hard
and he can spell *saxophone* backward."
"What?"

"But first, *señor,*" Papi says,
"we are gonna fill out your layaway form."
"Yessir!" the man says behind the counter
piled with used clarinets.

"How about
X
A
S
?

Sounds like 'YES'!
Short for *saxophone* — backward!!"
I say to the pawnshop music man.

"Uh — what?"
The man pops a clarinet
into a case.
"See? I told you,
Juanito's a smart boy!"
Papi says.

A day later
the bed is full of wood, sticks,
nails, and sandpaper.
"Just wait until I am done!"
Papi says with a green visor
on his head.

"You're gonna see something
when you get back from school tomorrow."
Papi spins to the kitchen
to get a cup of coffee. Then, he rolls back.
Carries wood, rushes back
to the kitchen table.

Mami hands him a saw.
"When I work, I work!"
Papi says, smiling.

I race home from
Bus #7.
Past the Rhythm Room.
Past Pep Boys
and Kessler's Messenger Service,
down the hall
past Doña Clementina Lucero Osorio's place,
turn left,
Door # 5.

Knock-knock, knockitty!
"Wait!" Mami says from inside.
"Come on, Mami!"
"Wait justa *minuto*," Papi says.
"Lemme put it on. . . ."
"Hurry, Felipe," Mami says.

Knock, knockitty-Knock!
"Can I come in now?"

"Ok, ok,
ok," Papi says.
"Close your eyes first . . .
ok?"
Step one.

Step two.
Step-step.

I squeeze my eyes.
I can see a little, but my eyelashes
make it look like I am inside
a cave with fuzzy spiders.

"One,
two,
three,
four,
cinco y yo brinco!"
Papi says.
"Jump!"

Open my eyes.
Looks like a giant Lady Bug
ready to hop over the El Cortez Hotel.
"What is that?" I ask.

"Escuteh!" Papi says.
"All the kids ride them at La Plazita!"
"A scooter!"
I leap up.
"For you, Juanito," Papi says.

"Of course, I'll beat you easy
if we have a race!"

"Oh yeah?"
I say, and roll the wooden scooter
to the front porch. The handlebars
are a capital *T* nailed down on
three capital *I*'s. Under the *I*'s
there's a pair of steel wheels in the front
and at the back another pair, smooth
as silver. Papi nailed soda bottle caps
in front of the capital *T.*
"Are these the headlights?"
"Correcto!" Papi says. "Are these little
skate wheels? Where did you get them?"

"Maria left them for you,
by her door. With this note
inside the skates," Papi says.

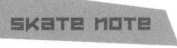

May 30

Hi, Frankie!
These skates are for you. Well, I hope
they fit you. Next time you move,
you can put these on and you'll get there faster!
Thanks for taking me to the beach.
Remember to keep away from strangers, ok!
And don't worry so much; your papi
said he's going to build you a scooter, and
then, guess what? He's going to bring you
to Tijuana! Be nice, ok!
Do I sound like a mean old sister? My father
says it's good that I am with Mama. She's alone
with my little brothers and sisters and needs help.
Even though I'll be selling chile powder, I'll
be practicing my English and going to school
at Alba Roja, downtown, right across
the street from Mama's work.

I won't ever forget you and your funny faces
and all your funny names. I like
Juanito the best.
Maybe I'll see you next summer
if you are still in #5.
Bye-bye, Frankie! Just kidding.

Maria #7

ONE, TWO, THREE!

I help Papi get to the sidewalk.
Mami rides my scooter a little.

"Ready?"
Mami says, counting down,
"One,
two,
and . . ."
she gives me the scooter.

My knuckles are white,
hands wrapped tight around the scooter handles.
One foot on the scooter wood board floor.
The other on the ground.
Sky so blue it looks like the sea.

"Are you the D Street scooter champion?"
Papi asks. "No, Papi," I say.

"No?"

"You are!"

¡Vámonos al perro!

June 1959

Mama Grande's Braids

Saturday comes.
Mami opens her pink jute bag
and unwraps Mama Grande's braids.

"I've been dragging these poor things
for the last nineteen years. It's time
to let them go, Juanito."
Mami folds them up and
burns them on the stove.

I open my toolbox,
take out my hammer
and the toy soldiers.
Line them up against the window
for everyone to see.
Some are broken.
It doesn't matter.

Mami takes Grandma Juanita's and
Grandpa Alejo's old brown photos from her bag.
"Let me see your hammer," she says.

Then, nails the frames on the wall
Above my sofa bed.

I look up at Grandpa Alejo
and Mama Grande Juanita.
Our room is a little smoky,
but — soon it will clear.

LESGO!

Mami says, "Lesgo!
It's Sunday!"

"*Vámonos!
Al perro!*" Papi says
after *huevos con papas* breakfast
with tortillas as big as the moon.

"But where are we going?" I ask.
"To the Greyhound," Mami says again.
"The hound? Why? Are we leaving?
I told you I don't want to move again!"
"You'll see, Juanito, *vas a ver,*" Mami says.

"I'll race you!"
"Well, to the door!" Papi says.

EL PERRO

"Remember to use
your automatic brakes!"
Papi says as he stops to catch his breath
at the Orpheum Theatre
on 8th and Broadway.

"What automatic brakes?"
"Your foot!"
Papi laughs.

I pass Walker Scott department store.
Inside the window — a woman
made out of white plaster
in a bikini and a plastic man smeared with
red plaster wearing Bermudas.
"Are those Bermudas?" I ask Papi behind me.
"See the cut-off pants?
I've heard of them on TV. You can wear those
and eat TV dinners! That's the latest thing!"
"What's a TV dinner?" Papi asks.

"It's a dinner that you put on top
of the TV in case you don't have
a table, right, Juanito?" Mami says,
winking her eye.

My scooter flies by La Plazita.
The winds are picking up.
Tree leaves race with us, too —
"Take me! Take me with you!"
they say as they spin-spin
by my heels.

FLYING UP

"Long time
we've been at D Street," Mami says.
"It almost feels like home."

We pass La Plazita, the three of us.
The pigeons are flying up.

There's a pair of doves
at the tip of the green dome
where little rivers flow down
into the fountain.
So still,
as if they have been there
all along.

Maybe I've been drooping
my head and only staring
at the little cracks on the sidewalk.

The sand-colored doves
open their wings and float
for a moment over me;
then they fly fast by my shoulders
up again, into the clouds.

They swoop down
for a second or two,
little angels, like Mami
and Papi, to drink the water that pours
out from the happy fountain.

IN THE MIDDLE OF THE STREET

We pass the Spreckles theater,
The *S* in rough glassy stars —
"Enrico Caruso performed there,"
Mami says. "I read it in the *Tribune*."

Cross the street —
Ocean's Lockers and Woody's Tattoo Parlour.
Dragons and eagles, anchors
and broken hearts painted on the wall.

I think of Chava in Mrs. Sniffins's class.
I think of Maria #7,
dusty Colonia Kilómetro 24, selling hot chile powder
in wrinkled paper bags.

This is Broadway Street. School's out.
In El Downtown. Not everybody comes this far
from Ramona Mountain or Logan Heights.

The middle of the street
is my favorite spot.
When I stand in the middle of the street,
I can feel the whole world move just a little.
Feel cars whir by, hear
steam machines whistle from the open

windows at Ocean's Lockers, hear sailors
shout down down from up there,
their white shirts glowing in the winds.

Here's my hand waving back, fluffy and fast.
Here's my feet rushing into the open aluminum doors
of the Greyhound station; Papi, behind me,
breathing hard,
on the wooden benches with Mami.

starry doors

Sit
in El Perro. The three of us.
Watch people go places.
Some with papers.
Some without.

"Come On, Let's Go!"
a fast, spicy song by Ritchie Valens
spins in the jukebox
by the chrome-bright candy store
and the magazine rack.

Shuffle there, sway
with the music.

The jukebox spills gold and red bows
of neon ribbon-light on my shirt.
It's as if the round guitar
is ringing inside of me
for the first time, inside,
next to my heart.
Mami and Papi on the bench
feel the music, too, I can tell,
because they are close to each other.
Papi taps one of his short round legs

on his chair while Mami
touches her cheek
as if to see if it is true, we are here
back where we started, somewhere
in a bus depot, in the early hours
when all the cats are gray.
Ritchie's guitar
shakes out the days
without Papi and nights wondering
if he will ever come back;
                    it melts
out of the
   whirling record
                    and the needle arm,
                         down the aisles,
                    to the starry doors
                         at the front;
      they swing
            back
      and
            forth,
                    back
      and
                                        forth;
the high,
   sweet
         guitar chords

float up,
going up
to the little wings of
doves and pigeons;
something
inside my chest
pours out, too, a river
that leads to green roads
and soft doors where we lived
with numbers and hallways;
then,
the river rises,
with its watery music,
its names, so many names that spell
my name and a hundred classrooms' names;
Aunt Faustina kisses the crystal eyes
of her worried dolls
and whispers, *buenas noches;*
Uncle Lalo comes home
with another machine
from the pawnshop, a tangled metal heart
he will fix back in Mexico, one day;
my cousins, they ride
the Ferris wheel at Playland
by the bay;
Chacho boxes a star; Aunt Albina
runs to the shore and cradles

a cup of sweet ocean water;
                                    Uncle Arturo
                    listens
                            to the sand tap its silver heels,
                                    kneels down, and records
                                            the electric waves;
                            Mami sits
                    with Papi
            in the long row of travelers
    to whoknowswhere, California;
it's almost 1960 —
    pretty soon, I'll be in sixth grade,
            my last year in elementary;
                    then, I'll start all over
                            in a new school
                    like always; it doesn't matter now;
            I am drinking warm water
from the faucet
    next to the photo booth,
            spilling some on my chest;
                    now, I am
                            in my little blue-gray *ranchito*
                    where everybody comes and goes
            with the morning moon flickering
    its last candle flame
            in the summer nights,
                    get little paper cups,

fill them up, by the singing creek,
    one for Papi,
        one for Mami,
                precious Papi,
         precious Mami,
      precious every moment —
  precious, like water.